A hurt horse

David stands in front of me, arms crossed. Buster pushes more of his weight against me, and I have to move my feet a little so he doesn't knock me over.

David stares at the pony, frowning. "How long has he been doing that?"

"See, there you go again, being Mr. Horse Expert," I said.

"Please, Josh," he says. "Is this why you took him out of the corral?"

"Duh! I tried to tell you that, remember?"

David slowly kneels, petting Buster's side. "Can I check this out?" he asks the pony, slowly moving his hands down Buster's left foreleg. When he reaches the hoof, Buster flinches and pulls away from David.

"Oh no," David groans.

Collect All the Vet Volunteers Books

Fight for Life

Homeless

Trickster

Manatee Blues

Say Good-bye

Storm Rescue

Teacher's Pet

Trapped

Fear of Falling

Time to Fly

Masks

End of the Race

New Beginnings

Acting Out

Helping Hands

LAURIE HALSE ANDERSON

Helping Hands

PUFFIN BOOKS
An Imprint of Penguin Group (USA) Inc.

PUFFIN BOOKS
An imprint of Penguin Young Readers Group
Published by the Penguin Group
Penguin Group (USA) Inc.
375 Hudson Street
New York, New York 10014, U.S.A.

USA / Canada / UK / Ireland / Australia / New Zealand / India / South Africa / China
Penguin Books Ltd, Registered Offices: 80 Strand, London WC2R 0RL, England

For more information about the Penguin Group visit www.penguin.com

First published in the United States of America by Puffin Books,
an imprint of Penguin Young Readers Group, 2013

LIBRARY OF CONGRESS CATALOGING-IN-PUBLICATION DATA IS AVAILABLE

Puffin Books ISBN 978-0-14-241677-8

Printed in the United States of America

1 3 5 7 9 10 8 6 4 2

Chapter One

I'm straightening up the hammer section in the back of my family's hardware store, Wrenches & Roses. A boring job? You bet, but Dad was so busy getting ready for this weekend's big sale that he just dumped the new shipment of hammers into one big bin.

If you ask me, there's not much difference between a claw hammer and a ball peen, but customers can be fussy. I sort them by type, and then by weight, and then by manufacturer. You never know: someone could walk into the store needing the perfect hammer. By the time I'm done, they'll be able to find it.

Dad calls out, "Check again, will you, Josh?"

I open the back door to check the alley and the parking lot. No sign of Gus, the pony handler. No ponies, either.

"Not yet," I say for the hundredth time.

Dad frowns, glances at the customers lining up outside the front door and then at the big clock on the wall. Gus stopped in a week ago when he saw our signs for the "Leap into Spring" sale. He showed us pictures of his two ponies, Buster and Babe. The names were cheesy, but the ponies were cute. Once my little sister, Sophie, saw them, she wouldn't let up.

"Please, Daddy, please?" she whined. "Ponies, ponies, ponies, ponies!"

Dad glanced at me and my twin sister, Jules, and asked what we thought.

"Free pony rides?" I asked. "The whole town will show up."

"It's a sure thing," Jules added.

After Dad booked Gus and the ponies, he ordered extra ads in the newspaper. Jules and I spent the last few days plastering all the telephone poles up and down Main Street with flyers: FREE PONY RIDES FOR KIDS AGES 8 AND UNDER. SATURDAY FROM 9 A.M. TO 2 P.M. SUNDAY FROM NOON TO 4 P.M.

The flyers and ads must have worked. We've

never had people in line waiting for the doors to open before. That's a beautiful sight.

We moved here from Pittsburgh after both of my parents were laid off. They had just enough in savings to buy this old store and fix it up, but money is really tight. Too many people want to shop at the big box stores instead of supporting local business, Mom explained. We haven't gotten our allowances in months, and we have to shop for new clothes at the thrift store, not the mall. Jules and I are the only kids in our grade who don't have cell phones. Last week I heard our parents talking about canceling our cable and Internet, which will completely ruin my life.

This weekend's big sale *has* to work.

Mom comes up from the basement carrying a small cardboard box, followed by Sophie, hopping around like Jules's pet rabbits, Cuddles and Lolli.

"Ponies, ponies! Pony rides today!" Sophie sings out. "Hip hip hooray, pony rides today!"

Mom double-checks the flower- and vegetable-seed display, filling in the missing packets. "Any sign, Josh?" she asks quietly.

I open the back door again. Still no Gus. Jules walks by me with a broom, her eyes wide and worried.

"Maybe he's stuck in traffic," I say, trying to sound more confident than I feel.

At the front of the store, Sophie presses her nose against the big glass door. "Look at all the kids," she says.

She's right—the line out there is getting longer.

"I still get the first ride, right, Daddy?" Sophie asks. "You promised."

Dad nods, but his smile is tight. "Did you try that number?" he asks Mom. "I put his card by the register."

"It's disconnected, honey," Mom says. "No matter how many times I call, that's not going to change."

Jules sweeps over to where I'm standing and whispers, "Do you think he stole Dad's money?"

"Shhh," I say, but I'm thinking that exact same thing. Gus had insisted that Dad pay him half of the appearance fee ahead of time, in cash. Dad was reluctant, but it was the only way Gus would agree to the deal. It's only a few minutes till opening time. Things look bad.

A heavy knock on the back door startles us all.

"Finally!" Dad says.

I rush to open it.

"It's just David," I announce. David Hutchinson

is one of the Vet Volunteers with Jules and me at Dr. Mac's veterinary clinic.

"Just David?" he repeats. "I deserve a little more credit than that, don't you think?"

He goes to throw a fake punch to my shoulder, but I shake my head.

"I'm not in the mood to play around," I say.

"What's wrong?" David asks, looking around. He smacks his forehead with the palm of his hand. "Is it the ponies? Did that guy bail on you?"

"Shhh," I warn. "Keep it down."

"Well, that's it," Dad says with a sigh. "Nine o'clock. We have to open."

"But—" I start.

Dad takes the big key ring off the counter and selects the key that will open the front door. "We don't have a choice, son."

Chapter Two

Wait!" Jules shouts. "I have an idea! We can stall them with Cuddles and Lolli until the ponies get here."

"How?" asks Mom.

"We can make a display in the middle of the store," Jules says. "Like a habitat."

"No," I say with a grin. "A *rabbitat*!"

David punches my shoulder and cracks up. Even Dad smiles.

"I'll show the kids how to handle them the right way," Jules says, "and try to teach them a little bit about caring for pets."

"Good idea," Mom agrees. "But make it fast!"

Dad opens the door and greets the first customers as the three of us—David, Jules, and me—set up some sections of plastic fence in the middle of the store. A few minutes later Jules, Cuddles, and Lolli are in the middle of the "rabbitat," ready to charm the children of Ambler.

It's a good thing Cuddles, the dwarf rabbit, has mellowed in the last few months. She's still very hoppy, of course. I mean, she is a rabbit after all. But since she's been spayed and Jules started to train her, Cuddles doesn't chew on as many non-toys as she used to. She'll sit still longer when you're petting her, too, probably because Lolli (who is so big she should be called the Bunny Beast) tires her out every day.

The first group of little kids enters into the rabbitat. Cuddles sits up on her hind legs, twitching her floppy ears and sniffing the air before hopping over to them and lying down to be petted. As Jules shows the kids what to do, Cuddles tugs and nibbles on one boy's shoelace.

"Hey!" he giggles.

"Okay Cuddles, that's enough," Jules says, distracting her from the shoelace with a pink chew toy.

Mom sets up a small activity table with paper and crayons to keep the other kids busy while they're waiting to pet the bunnies—well, waiting, actually, to ride a pony. People wander around the store, browsing. A few pick up things like seed packets and light bulbs, but those don't cost very much. Mom and Dad look more than nervous; they're scared. Maybe our money situation is even worse than I thought. If the ponies don't show up, we're in big trouble.

"Are you going to tell me what's going on," David asks, "or do I have to ask Jules?"

I motion for David to follow me out the back door. The parking lot is empty because this is where the pony rides are supposed to be. I quickly bring David up to date on the growing disaster.

"What if he never shows up?" David asks.

Before I can answer, Gus pulls his beat-up old truck and rusty red horse trailer into the parking lot. He parks behind the row of planters that Mom filled with flowers and herbs. The driver's-side door of the truck creaks open but gets stuck half-way. Gus kicks it, shouting a few words that are definitely not kid-friendly. He better not talk like that around Sophie.

Gus finally gets out of his truck and spits on the ground. "Pipe corral's back there." He points to the bed of the pickup. "You two stop staring and unload. I'll get the ponies." He doesn't wait for an answer, just walks to the back end of the horse trailer, grumbling to himself.

The truck, the trailer, and Gus all look like they've seen better days.

"Man," David mutters. "I hope he's nicer to the ponies than he is to people."

"At least he's here," I say. "Let me run in and tell my folks, then I'll help unload."

Everyone in the store cheers when I announce that the ponies have arrived and the rides will begin soon. My dad cheers the loudest, his face relieved.

I hurry back outside. David hands the panels of the corral to me one at a time. They're made out of hollow metal pipes, so they aren't too heavy, but they are kind of awkward. I'm not exactly sure what to do with them. Luckily, David knows, probably from all the time he spends at Quinn's horse stables.

"Do you want us to set up all eight of these for one enclosure?" David calls to Gus.

"Yeah," Gus grumbles from inside the trailer.

"What's he doing?" I ask.

"Probably undoing the pony's lead," David explains.

Gus backs a stocky pony out of the trailer. She has a creamy grayish coat and a solid gray mane and tail. It looks like she's wearing short white socks on three of her legs. On the front right leg, the white goes all the way up to her knee, like she put the wrong sock on.

"Must be Babe," I say. She looks older and more worn out than the pony photos that Gus showed us. Maybe it's not even the same animal.

Jules and Sophie lead a line of kids to the parking lot and get them to sit down and watch us finish unloading the panels. They're so excited that they can barely sit still.

Gus drops the lead of the gray pony. "Wait there, Babe," he says gruffly.

Babe turns her rump to him and plops a big pony poop near his feet. The little kids squeal and shout. Then she lifts one of her front legs up and clomps it on the asphalt, like she's counting. Sophie and the little kids start clapping.

"Why is she doing that?" I ask David.

"Maybe she's hungry," he replies.

Sure enough, Babe takes two steps toward Mom's planters and starts munching on the brightly colored zinnias.

"Whoa there, girl!" David runs to Babe, pats her neck, and picks up her lead. Then he gently walks her away from the plants and ties her to the first corral panel. Babe yawns, showing huge boxy teeth, and shakes her gray mane, which makes the kids squeal even louder.

When David kneels to connect the corral panels, Babe heads back toward the planters, dragging the panel she's tied to behind her. This time she starts in on the young basil plants.

"Oh no, you don't!" I say.

I don't really have any experience with horses, but I run over and grab the lead. The basil plants are already gone, and Babe has started in on the dill, crunching loudly.

"Just give her a gentle tug," David calls.

"Dill's gross," I mutter to the pony as I pull on her lead. "You really don't want to eat that."

She tosses her head, and her forelock falls to the side, revealing splotches of white on her forehead, face, and muzzle, and deep brown eyes with long eyelashes. She snorts through her big furry nostrils, then stares up at me. She's got a little wrinkle of creamy gray and white fur at the edge of her mouth that reminds me of Sophie's dimples. It's almost as if the pony is smiling at me and planning more mischief.

"No," I warn, "we don't have time for fooling around."

Babe sniffs at me, then tilts her head and makes a funny noise vibrating her lips like she's blowing me a raspberry.

"Forget it," I say. "No more plants. Mom is going to flip out when she sees what you've already done."

"Come on, Josh," David calls. "I need your help."

We tie Babe to the first two panels that he pinned together. They should be too heavy for her to move, but I keep an eye on her, just in case.

Chapter Three

David makes putting the corral together look easy.

"You connect the panels with the metal pins, like this. See?" he asks. "Do those over there the same way. It should look like an octagon once it's finished."

I try to pin two panels together and manage to drop everything. It's a good thing David's here to help. The kids in line are getting impatient, and Gus still hasn't gotten the second pony out of the trailer. All we can hear is his muffled voice and a lot of pony stomping and clomping. It doesn't sound like either one of them is happy.

"That guy is not very good with horses," David

says, concerned. "No wonder it doesn't want to come out."

We finally finish pinning the corral panels and weigh them down with heavy sandbags from the truck. I'm sweating from all the unexpected work.

"Do you have a gate?" David calls to Gus.

"Do you *see* a gate?" Gus snarls.

David makes a face at me. "We'll leave a little space between those last two panels for kids to get in and out of the corral."

By now, a crowd of people has gathered in the parking lot. Jules is trying to keep the little kids entertained, but a couple of them have started to fidget.

"Do we need to put a saddle on her or anything?" I ask David.

"Of course," David says. "How else are the kids going to ride?"

I don't really want to explain to him that I know absolutely nothing about ponies. Or horses. I'm not even sure what the difference is.

A noisy commotion in the horse trailer saves me from having to answer him.

Gus squeezes out the side door of the trailer and kicks the door closed. "Dog meat!" he shouts. "You're gonna be dog meat if you don't back your rump out of there!"

"Hey there, Mr. Gus," I say loudly, hoping none of the little kids heard what he just said.

David must be thinking the same thing. He jogs over to the trailer. "May I try?" he asks.

"Suit yourself," Gus grumbles. "That pony's so stubborn, he might as well be a mule." Gus stalks over to the far end of the parking lot and lights a cigarette.

David pokes his head in the trailer window. "Hey there, boy," he says gently. "Having a rough time this morning? I would be, too, if I were stuck in this stinky trailer." He turns and whispers to me, "This trailer is disgusting. Looks like it hasn't been cleaned out in months."

I don't know what to say to that. I'm in way over my head. I mean, I love animals, but I've only ever been around little ones, like bunnies and cats. Ponies or horses—whatever—they're way bigger than bunnies and cats. They seem to be a lot more trouble, too.

David strokes the brown and white pony through the window. "Let's see if we can get you out here in the fresh air. Come on, buddy." He turns to me. "Can you get some carrots or maybe an apple? We can use them to lure him out."

Now there's something I can help with. I run past Babe, go inside the store, and snag some of

Cuddles and Lolli's carrots. But it's no use. Buster still won't move, not even for a yummy treat.

"Horses and ponies are creatures of habit," David says. "And some don't like walking backward. I helped Mr. Quinn's horse, Trickster, get used to his trailer. He didn't like going in or out, either. Maybe Babe can help us out. Josh, bring her over here."

"Me?" I ask.

"I don't think Gus is going to help, do you?"

I swallow hard and hope David doesn't realize how nervous I am. Babe watches me carefully as I untie her lead. "Just don't bite me, okay?" I whisper. Once she's untied, I walk her to the trailer, and her hooves *clip-clop* on the asphalt behind me. She smells horsey: dusty and sweaty, with a hint of hay and Mom's basil. Suddenly, she head-butts me right in the middle of my back and almost sends me crashing to the ground.

"What the heck are you kids up to?" Gus shouts from across the parking lot. "I already got that one out."

"Buster shakes every time that dude yells," David says, annoyed. "It's okay, buddy, look, here comes Babe."

I hand him her lead and rub my back. "Careful. She thinks she's a goat."

"Yeah, I saw that," David says. "I think she likes you."

David leads Babe back into the trailer. The two ponies nuzzle each other's necks, and Buster lets out a big sigh.

"Okay then," David says. "Let's try this again." He clicks his tongue. "That's it, Buster. Just do like Babe is doing. Easy does it."

And sure enough, David manages to coax Buster to follow in Babe's footsteps and back out of the trailer. "Good boy, Buster! That wasn't so bad now, was it?"

Buster snorts and looks around the parking lot, taking everything in: the corral, the back of the store, the Dumpster, and the line of excited kids sitting with Jules, their parents standing behind them. He keeps looking back to Babe, as if he wants her to tell him that everything is going to be okay.

I understand the feeling totally.

Buster has a small white star of fur on his forehead and a white patch on his muzzle, like Babe's. His coat is a pretty combination of reddish-brown and white patches, but it's matted down and dirty. His white legs are splattered with dried mud and manure. I was hoping that Buster would be younger and perkier than Babe, but he's even more of a mess.

David notices, too.

"Hey buddy," he says, touching the pony's tangled mane. "When was the last time you were groomed?" He pats Buster on the head and the pony shies a bit. "It's okay, we'll take care of you."

David tells me to lead Babe into the pipe corral, and he follows right behind with Buster. The waiting kids clap, and Sophie starts singing her pony song again.

"Thank you. Thank you." David bows to the crowd and hams it up. "I'm a certified horse genius, if I do say so myself."

"Ha," I say. "I wouldn't go that far, but you don't completely stink at pony handling." I punch his shoulder, not too hard, just friendly. This could have been a nightmare without his help.

"Ow, ow, ow!" David rubs his shoulder and fakes that he's in pain. "You're just jealous of my amazing horse-taming skills."

I try to smile because he's just teasing, but the truth is I *am* jealous. It's like David was born to deal with these ponies. Jules is a natural with rabbits—that's why we call her the Bunny Whisperer. At Dr. Mac's clinic, Maggie's in charge of dogs, Sunita is the cat expert, and Brenna, well, she's the nature girl who connects with all the wild critters. I like animals, too, but I don't have special skills the way they do. In fact, I'm not sure I should be a Vet Volunteer at all.

Gus slams the back door of the trailer closed. Buster startles and pulls at his lead rope.

"Whoa there, buddy," David says. "Everything's fine." Buster relaxes as David pets his neck. "You should have seen me with Trickster," David says. "He was terrified of the trailer because he'd been in an accident in one. He's a lot bigger and more powerful than these old ponies. He's more than sixteen hands high."

"Hands?" I ask, confused.

"Horses are measured in hands, didn't you know that? Each hand is four inches. Buster and Babe are maybe ten hands high. You weren't here at Thanksgiving, were you? I got to ride Trickster in the Ambler Thanksgiving parade. We looked pretty good, if I do say so myself. But you should really see my dad's horse, King's Shadow—"

"Let's get the pony rides started," I interrupt. "You can tell me that other stuff later."

Mom pops her head out the back door and calls to me. "How's it going out here?"

"Great," I smile and wave. "We're just about ready."

Babe lifts one foot in the air like she is waving, too. Mom smiles and goes back in. Good thing she didn't notice what Babe ate for breakfast.

Chapter Four

Where's the grooming gear?" David asks Gus.

Gus grunts and jerks his thumb toward the trailer.

"Wait, what are you doing?" I ask, following David.

"We have to groom Buster."

"No, we don't. Look at all those kids. We need to get the saddles on."

David takes a faded plastic crate out of the back of the trailer and carries it to the corral. "Nobody rides until the ponies are ready."

I had no idea it was going to be this complicated. Gus should have showed up two hours early instead of half an hour late.

David pulls a weird-looking thing the size of a hockey puck out of the crate.

"This is a currycomb," he says, working it through Buster's coat. "You need to groom them, especially here, where the saddle goes. If you don't pick out the burs and stickers, they'll really hurt once the rider is on."

He trades the currycomb for a brush. "Most horses like to be groomed. Look how Buster is leaning into this. He's already happier, which will make the pony rides safer for the kids. No one wants to ride a cranky pony."

Some of the kids in line are whining. I hear some parents grumbling, too, until Jules drowns them out by starting a sing-along to "Old MacDonald Had a Hardware Store."

Buster looks a whole lot better after he's been brushed. I comb his mane clean while David starts on Babe. By the time I'm done, Buster stands a little taller, as if he knows he looks better and he's proud of it.

"Anytime now!" an impatient dad calls from the long line of waiting kids.

David carries the saddles and bridles from the truck as I'm finishing Babe's mane. I watch as he sets the saddles over the saddle pads and cinches up the girths. "Tacking up," he calls it. The ponies take the bits in their mouths, and the bridles are buckled up around their jaws.

"There's a mounting block in the back of the truck," Gus calls.

David and I lift it down together and set it up inside the corral so kids can climb on and off the ponies.

"Not that I mind," David says, "but isn't that guy supposed to be doing all this?"

"He is," I say. "But the whole point of the pony rides is to bring families to the store and to keep their kids happy. I think Gus would scare them all away." I pause. "Look, you've already helped a lot and I really appreciate it, but you don't have to stay if you don't want to."

"You're kidding me, right?" David stands. "Helping is what the Vet Volunteers are all about. We have to, or we face the wrath of Dr. Mac." He grins so I know he's joking. "My dad can't pick me up until later this afternoon, and you could use a hand, so . . . can I stay?"

It's my turn to grin.

"The Wrenches and Roses First Annual Pony Ride is officially open," I shout. "Who's first?"

Sophie sprints across the parking lot before I can say another word, and David helps her onto Babe's saddle. Sophie is singing as loudly as she can. I hope David's grooming made Babe happy enough that she won't mind the off-key tune.

I hang back, unsure what to do.

"Go ahead," David urges. "That little guy at the front of the line, I think his name is Malik. He was in my sister's class last year. Pick him up and put him on Buster."

"Right," I say, trying to look more confident than I feel.

I wave Malik over, and he runs to the corral and jumps up onto the mounting block. Buster stands perfectly still while I help Malik into the saddle. He shuffles his feet a bit as the little boy pats his neck.

David has already walked Sophie and Babe half-way around the corral. "Go ahead," he calls. "Take his lead."

I lead Buster and Malik slowly around the corral. Both boy and pony seem to be having fun. So far, so good.

David and I lead the pony rides for the next hour, while Gus sleeps in a folding chair with his hat over his face. Jules helps by entertaining the kids in line. The kids are all happy, and their parents are smiling. I cross my fingers and hope that means they'll turn into Wrenches & Roses customers.

"So when was the last time you rode a horse?" David asks, once we've both settled into the routine.

"Um . . . never," I admit.

"Never?" he asks. "*Never*, as in, not once in your entire life?"

"Yeah, that's usually what 'never' means."

"Man"—he pats Buster's neck—"I don't know if I could handle that."

"If you'd never been on a horse, you probably wouldn't think it was such a big deal," I point out.

"I can't remember a time when I wasn't on a horse," he says. "My dad was supposed to go to the Olympics, but it got canceled that year. We have pictures of me riding with him when I was two years old."

"My dad taught me how to play soccer," I say, even though it isn't exactly the truth.

"That's cool," David says. "Dad and I are going riding tomorrow. He'll be on King's Shadow. When my dad is riding him, it looks like the two of them are flying."

"I help my dad with the store a lot," I say. "You know, the family business."

I'm secretly wishing that my dad could afford a horse, or that he had the time to take me to the stables, or a soccer field, or anywhere.

"You have to work here a lot, don't you?" David asks.

I'm saved from the need to answer him by Maggie and Zoe, who walk up to the corral, grinning and checking out our work with the ponies. They're both granddaughters of Dr. Mac, our town veterinarian and the leader of the Vet Volunteers. Maggie's lived with Dr. Mac since she was a baby, and now Zoe lives with them, too, since her mom is an actress working in Hollywood.

"Looks like you have this under control," Maggie says.

"Thanks to David," Jules says. She's left the line of kids under the watchful eye of a mom with a baby in her arms.

Zoe rolls her eyes. "Don't say that too loud—you'll make his head swell even bigger."

That makes David laugh. Babe swishes her tail like she's joining him.

"Did you guys hear about Ranger?" Maggie asks.

"Mr. Fedor's dog?" I ask. I haven't met him yet, but the other volunteers say he's a nice old man whose dog, Ranger, is always getting into trouble.

"What happened this time?" David asks.

"He tried to make friends with a porcupine," Maggie says.

I wince. “Ouch!”

“Totally,” Zoe agrees.

“Poor Ranger,” Jules says. “Is he going to be okay?”

“Nothing keeps Ranger down,” Maggie says. “Gran said the hardest part was removing the quills stuck in his nose. He won’t go near a porcupine again, that’s for sure.”

Just then, Buster lifts his tail and leaves a huge pile of poop on the parking lot.

“Ewww!” says the little girl riding him. I’m thinking the same thing, but I try not to show it. Pony poop smells even grosser than it sounds.

“I’ll get the shovel,” says Jules.

“This is the perfect time for us to leave,” Maggie says, laughing. “Remember, guys, the clinic closed at noon today. Gran is taking us camping on the Lehigh River.”

“Sounds like fun,” I say.

“Not really. We have to sleep in a tent,” says Zoe, wrinkling her nose. “On the ground.”

Zoe is more of a hotel kind of girl. A five-star hotel, if you please. With room service and a view.

“What about the animals?” I ask.

“Ranger went home with Mr. Fedor last night. Gran’s been planning this camping horror for months, so we don’t have any boarders,” Zoe says. "Sherlock Holmes is staying with a guy from Gran's book club and Socrates will be very happy to have twenty-four hours of peace and quiet."

The first time I met Sherlock Holmes, Dr. Mac's old basset hound, he drooled so much on my sneakers that I had to change my socks when I got home. Socrates, the clinic's cat, still won't let me get close enough to pet him. Maybe he senses that I'm not sure if I really belong with the group.

"Is Dr. Gabe on call?" David asks.

Dr. Gabe is the other vet who works with Dr. Mac.

Maggie nods. "He's at a conference in Philly right now," she says. "But he'll be back tonight."

"Gotta go, cousin," Zoe says. "I'm not done packing. Gran says all we need are old T-shirts and shorts, but I think my clothes should match even if we're in the middle of nowhere."

Maggie rolls her eyes. Zoe loves fashion. Maggie, not so much. Zoe likes to cook bizarre, healthy foods that smell gross and taste worse, while Maggie is a pizza, burgers, and wings girl. As far as I could tell, the only thing they have in common, besides their grandmother, is that they care about animals more than anything else.

"Just remember, you have to carry what you pack," Maggie says. "See you guys. Have fun!"

"This would be a great weekend to go camping," David says. "My dad's taking me to the Chester County Horse Show tomorrow. You want to come with us?"

"I can't," I say. "The ponies are going to be here tomorrow, too. It looks like Jules and I are going to be stuck working."

The words come out meaner than I'd planned, but the truth is, I'm getting a little fed up with David's bragging about his horse experience and his father.

Out on Main Street a car revs its engine and beeps its horn loudly. Buster startles, almost jerking the lead out of my hands.

"Hold tight," David calls. "If you're calm, he'll be calm."

I won't miss David's bragging tomorrow, but I sure will miss his help. I hope Jules and I can handle it.

Chapter Five

Soon another Vet Volunteer, Brenna Lake, shows up with her younger brother, Jayvee. You'd think Jayvee wouldn't be very excited about boring ponies. He gets to hang out with all kinds of wild critters because his family runs a nature preserve and wild animal rehab center. But Jayvee is as horse-crazy as all the other kids, leaning forward to hug Buster and wave at Brenna, who is watching outside the corral with Edgar Allan Poe Crow on her shoulder.

Yup, a crow. A real, live crow. I didn't believe it the first time I saw it.

Brenna gives Jules a hug. "This is so cool you have ponies here in the middle of town! I haven't seen Jayvee this excited since winter vacation."

Jules grins and hugs her back. I'm glad my sister is finally making friends. We moved here in the middle of the school year, and things were bumpy for her, especially with Maggie. Life got a lot better once we joined the Vet Volunteers, although Jules has had an easier time fitting in with the group than me.

"How often do these ponies get a break?" Brenna asks as I help Jayvee off Buster. "And when was the last time they had any food or water?"

Brenna has strong opinions about how animals should be treated, and she isn't shy about sharing them.

"They've only been here a couple hours," I explain. "Do they really need a break? We still have kids waiting for a ride."

"Brenna's right," David says, "though I hate to admit it. I should have been paying more attention. They need a water break now."

"Did they eat before you started working them?" Brenna asks, staring at me as intensely as her crow does.

David glances at Gus, snoring in the shade. "Wouldn't surprise me if they're hungry, too," he admits.

Jayvee tugs on Brenna's arm. "I'm hungry," he says.

"My mom has sandwiches and juicc inside for anyone under ten," I say.

"Perfect," Brenna says. She turns to the parents and kids waiting in the line. "The ponies need a short break, folks."

"We have snacks in the store for you. And lots of stuff on sale, too," I add lamely. "Be sure to check out the hammer display."

While David shows me how to loosen the saddle cinch under the ponies' bellies, I ask him what they normally eat.

"Fresh hay two or three times a day," he says, "plus plenty of water, as long as they're not hot from running around." He ties Buster's lead to the corral with a fancy knot. "Depending on the horse, it might get grain or special food. You need a salt lick, too, for the minerals."

I try to tie Babe's lead rope in the same kind of knot that David did. "How much hay?"

"About four tons a year."

"What? That's eight thousand pounds!" I say.

"Wow, you're good at math," David says.

"Do they poop four tons a year, too?" I ask, eyeing the growing manure pile by the Dumpster.

"Sure seems like it sometimes. No, don't take the saddle off, this is just a break."

Babe flicks her ears, trying to shoo away the fly buzzing above her head.

"What do we do now?" I ask.

David gestures toward Gus. "I hate to do it, but we have to wake up Sleeping Beauty."

I groan, but we don't have a choice. I lead the way across the parking lot to where the pony handler is snoozing. "Excuse me," I say. "Um, Gus? Hello?"

Gus just snores.

"Wake up!" shouts David.

Gus snorts, jerks, and flings his hat to the ground. "What's wrong with you two, hollering at a fella like that?"

Sleeping Grumpy is more like it.

"Sorry," I say sheepishly. "Where can we find your water bucket and the hay for the ponies?"

"Isn't this a hardware store?" Gus stretches and stands. "Get a bucket in there."

"What about the hay?" I ask. "What are we supposed to feed them?"

"Those old ponies ain't hungry yet," Gus says. "They're used to working all day without food."

"That's not good for them," David says.

"Let them nibble on that grass back there." Gus points his chin at the narrow patch of green beyond the back of the parking lot. "Stay with them, though. Don't want to go chasing after them. I'm going in search of a hot lunch and a drink."

And with that, he ambles off toward Main Street.

"What a jerk," David says. "Now what?"

"I'll get a water bucket from the store," I say. "Mom and Dad won't mind, I hope. Do you believe what he said about the ponies not needing to eat anything?"

"No," David says. "Any chance you have hay bales or horse feed in the store?"

My imagination gallops away for a second. I picture Wrenches & Roses expanding with a barn built in this lot filled with feed, saddles, and anything else a horse might want.

"Josh? Did you hear me?" David asks, waving his hand in front of my eyes. "We need to feed these guys. Me, too. I'm starving."

I blink and snap out of it. "I hope they like carrots."

A few minutes later I stagger back out to the parking lot carrying two heavy buckets of water, with a plastic bag of carrots dangling from my mouth. David is upstairs in our kitchen raiding the refrigerator with Jules. I'm hungry, too, but this might be my only chance to see if I can be a Vet Volunteer without David showing me how to do everything.

Buster shakes his head, whinnying loudly, when he sees me.

I stop, shocked, and the bag of carrots falls to the ground. Buster is the only pony in the corral!

Babe is back at Mom's planter boxes, calmly munching marigolds. I must have messed up the knot on her lead. Or maybe that pony is a magician. No, I messed up the knot. I'll get David to help me convince her to head back to the corral.

Buster whinnies again and crosses the corral, staring at the water buckets and the bag of treats. He's definitely hungry. And thirsty. So Babe must be feeling the same way . . .

I set one bucket inside the corral. Buster slurps so loudly that Babe stops chewing to watch him.

"That's it, girl." I hold out the second bucket. "This one is just for you. Come and get it."

She ignores me and goes back to demolishing the marigolds. I can't carry the water and grab for her lead, so I put the bucket down and walk toward her slowly. Just when I'm almost close enough to reach her lead rope, she trots away to the farthest planter, filled with red, white, and blue petunias.

"Argh!" I know I should use a gentle but firm voice, like David did to coax Buster out of the trailer, but I just want to stomp my foot and scream. Babe looks at me, blue petunias dangling from her mouth. I swear she's laughing at me.

"Come *on*, Babe." If David and Jules walk out and see me making a fool of myself like this, I'll never hear the end of it. "Please, I'm begging you!"

Babe sighs, turns, and heads toward the corral, trotting faster than she's moved all morning.

Yes! I did it!

Just then Jules come out the back door carrying a couple of huge plastic bags, followed by David, who is balancing two paper plates loaded with sandwiches and potato chips. The door slams closed behind him. The sudden noise startles Babe so much that she swerves and bolts for the busy traffic on Main Street.

"*No!*" I scream.

Chapter Six

Jules moves as fast as I do; she heads left and I head right. It's the twin thing at work again, the weird connection between us that pops up at the strangest times. We don't need to talk, which is good because we don't have time. We circle around the pony until we're both standing on the sidewalk in front of her, our arms out to our sides.

A few cars honk their horns. Babe shakes her mane at the noise. She looks scared and confused by all the commotion.

I slowly raise my arms. "Talk to her," I tell my sister. "Calmly. We have to distract her."

Jules mirrors what I'm doing with my arms. "I talk rabbit, not horse."

"Fake it," I say. "That's what I'm doing." I step toward the pony. Babe snorts and paws at the ground with her hoof.

"Should I call nine one one?" shouts a driver.

Any second now my parents are going to come outside, or this pony is going to run into the street and cause an accident or get hurt, or the police will come, or maybe all those things will happen at the same time.

Babe snorts again.

"What is she doing?" Jules asks.

A loud whinny came from the middle of our parking lot. All of us—Jules, Babe, and I—stop and stare.

David grins and whinnies again, sounding exactly like a horse. He walks toward the runaway pony, half a peanut butter sandwich in each hand. "Come and get it, beautiful," he says confidently.

Babe paws at the ground, twitching her nose.

Jules and I exchange a glance and step forward at the same time.

David makes a clicking noise with his tongue. Babe takes a step toward David, then stops, looking back at Jules and me, and then at David again.

"Go on," I say softly. "Go get your treat."

"Peanut butter," David says. "Yum!"

Babe's nose twitches again, her eyes focused on

the food. I take another step closer. Jules does the same thing. I'm close enough to reach out and grab her lead, but David shakes his head.

"Don't!" he warns. "Let her come to me."

Sure enough, Babe trots straight to David, and as she takes the sandwich from him, he wraps her lead rope around his hand. After she's finished eating the first half of the sandwich, he holds the second half just in front of her nose and walks her into the corral. He rewards her with the rest of the sandwich and pats her head.

"Can you bring over the water bucket?" he asks.

As soon as I set the full water bucket in the corral, Babe plunges her head into it and slurps, then she lifts her head up and shakes hard, soaking me. David manages to jump back just in time to stay dry, laughing.

"You need some horse sense, Josh!"

I bend down and pretend to retie my sneaker, my face burning. Yeah, he's good with horses, I get it, and I know better than anyone that I'm clueless about Babe and Buster. But he doesn't have to keep rubbing it in.

Jules fetches the plastic bags she dropped when she chased after Babe.

"What's that?" I ask.

She rips open the plastic. "Timothy hay," she

says. "It's what Cuddles and Lolli eat, but hay is hay, right, David? The other bag has alfalfa pellets for small animals, but I figured the ponies wouldn't mind."

"Did you ask Mom if you could take those?" I ask.

"Why should I?" Jules answers. "It's our store."

"Exactly, that's why we're supposed to sell things, not steal them."

"The ponies are hungry, Josh," she says.

"I know, I know." Sometimes I think Jules doesn't understand the way the business runs. Or maybe she doesn't want to know. Twins have more differences than most people realize. "I know you're not a thief, but . . ."

"Yeah." She hands me the bag of alfalfa pellets. "Here, you feed them; it'll make you feel better."

The ponies had been chewing the small piles of Timothy hay, but as soon as I dig into the alfalfa bag, they stop and crowd around me.

"Whoa," I say, "take it easy, you two."

Jules takes the bag and pours alfalfa pellets into my hands, which I hold out to the hungry ponies. I've never fed any horses or ponies before, but there's no time to be nervous. They eat right out of my hands, their whiskers tickling my palms and making me laugh.

"Cup your hands more," David says. "You don't want them to bite your fingers."

"You don't have to explain everything to him," Jules says.

I smile at her, and she winks. With everything that's gone wrong today, it's nice to know that somebody has my back.

The line of riders is forming again, so after another handful of pellets and a drink, we tighten the cinches on the ponies' saddles. While David puts the bridle on Babe, I slip the bridle over Buster's head. Somehow I manage to get it on properly, much to my surprise.

The line is shorter than it had been in the morning, so we let the kids stay on the ponies longer. Babe circles the corral much faster than Buster, almost like she's in the mood for racing, or he's decided to be a turtle.

"If you lead him any slower, you'll be standing still," David says as he and Babe pass us again.

"It's him, not me," I say. "Do you think he needs a nap?"

"He's just jealous he didn't get a peanut butter sandwich," David says. "You wouldn't believe the special food that Olympic horses get. My dad said . . ."

I tune him out. All he wants to talk about is his

amazing father and what a good rider he is, and all the cool things they're going to do this summer, like riding horseback in the mountains of Virginia and giving jumping lessons at Quinn's stables and going to Disneyworld, and on and on and on. Summer vacation is only a month away, but I'm not exactly looking forward to it. For Jules and me, it's going to be a summer of babysitting Sophie and helping at the store. If we're lucky, we'll be able to squeeze in a few hours a week at Dr. Mac's clinic.

Buster and I stop at the mounting block to change riders, and he leans against me. Five minutes later, he does it again. His head is drooping, too, and he's walking even slower.

I interrupt David in the middle of a story about how the British royal family flies its horses in luxury airplanes.

"Something's not right," I say.

"What did you say?" David asks.

"I don't think he wants any more riders," I say.

David laughs and points at me. "You mean, *you* don't want to walk around this corral anymore."

"No, seriously," I say. "He's acting weird. I'll lead Babe if you want, but Buster is done for the day."

"Maybe he's sore from walking on the asphalt."

David pauses and studies the pony. "It's almost two, right? I'll finish up here with Babe. Why don't you let him graze on that grass back there? Just make sure he doesn't run away."

I quickly remove Buster's saddle and lead him out of the corral. We detour to fill the water bucket, but to my surprise, he doesn't drink very much. Even more puzzling, he's not interested in grazing at all.

"Man, I wish you could talk," I tell him as I scratch behind his ears. He looks at me with mournful eyes, and I wonder if he's thinking the same thing about me.

It's peaceful out here. The sun is high and hot. Bees buzz in the clover, and from far away I hear the jingle of the ice-cream truck. Buster stands next to me, his eyes on the ground. He doesn't raise his head for anything, not even when David brings Babe over.

"Two o'clock," he says. "Day's over!"

Babe lowers her head to munch on the grass, her tail gently swatting at a few flies. Buster still hasn't moved.

"Did you two enjoy your little rest?" David asks.

Part of me knows he's just teasing. The other part is fed up.

"Knock it off," I say.

"What?" David asks.

"You know what."

"No, I don't. What are you talking about?" He looks at me like he's honestly confused, but I don't believe it.

"You've been showing off all day," I say. "I get it: you know horses. You know everything about horses, and your dad does, too, and I'm an idiot. You've said it all a hundred times; now will you just shut up?"

"Dude, I was just kidding," he protests.

"No, you weren't. I think something is wrong with Buster, and yeah, I don't know as much as you do about ponies or horses or whatever they are, but you've been treating me like I'm lazy or stupid or something. I don't like it."

I stop, clenching my jaw, because a lot of other feelings are bubbling up, things that have nothing to do with David but that have been bugging me for a long time. I feel like punching something or crying or doing both, but if I did anything like that in front of him, I'd feel even worse.

Buster leans against me again, as if he knows how much I need a friend right now.

"Go," I tell David. "Just go. Thanks for your help. I'll clean everything up before Gus gets back."

David stands in front of me, arms crossed. Buster pushes more of his weight against me, and I have to move my feet a little so he doesn't knock me over.

David stares at the pony, frowning. "How long has he been doing that?"

"See, there you go again, being Mr. Horse Expert," I said.

"Please, Josh," he says. "Is this why you took him out of the corral?"

"Duh! I tried to tell you that, remember?"

David slowly kneels, petting Buster's side. "Can I check this out?" he asks the pony, slowly moving his hands down Buster's left foreleg. When he reaches the hoof, Buster flinches and pulls away from David.

"Oh no," David groans.

Chapter Seven

Oh no, what?" I ask.

"I don't know exactly," David admits, "but he won't let me check his shoe. This leg is warm, and look"—he points—"it's a little swollen between his hoof and knee."

"Is that why he was leaning on me?" I ask.

David nods. "I bet it hurts to put weight on that leg." He checks the other hooves. "I'm an idiot," he mutters.

"What did you just say?"

He stands up, shaking his head. "I should have checked their hooves this morning when we groomed them. I thought about it, but those kids, they wanted to ride, and I figured the ponies only had to walk around in circles a couple times." He pauses and looks me in the eye. "And then we got so busy that I forgot."

"It's not exactly your fault," I say. "It's Gus's responsibility to take care of them."

"Yeah, but obviously he's not doing that." He sticks his hands in the back pockets of his jeans. "I should have taken the time to do it right. I hate this feeling."

"What feeling?" I ask.

"Like I want to punch myself in the face for being so stupid. You probably want to punch me, too; I gave you a hard time about slacking, and you were just trying to help Buster."

"Um." I'm not sure what I'm supposed to say. "If it will make you feel better, I can punch you in the face, but that's not going to help Buster. What do you think is wrong?"

"Could be a lot of things." He pats Buster's shoulder and crouches in front of the bad leg again. "You should feel the heat coming off this part of his leg."

"How do you know he won't kick you?" I ask, nervously eyeing the pony's sharp hooves.

David brushes his hair out of his eyes. "If I tell you, will you accuse me of showing off again?"

"I won't, I promise."

"Cool," he says. "Buster will tell you before he kicks. You just have to speak his language, his body language. First, he'll put his ears back and bare his teeth. If you don't pay attention to that, he'll turn his rear end toward you and lift a back leg. You see a back leg come up? Get the heck out of the way, because you're about to be kicked."

I double-check; Buster's back feet are firmly planted on the ground.

"Do you want to feel the leg now?" David asks.

I'd rather rearrange the hammer display, but Buster looks up at me and it feels like he's saying I should try. He has a point. It's the only way I can learn how to help.

I swallow hard and kneel in the warm grass.

"Start with your hand on his shoulder and move it down slowly, so he understands what you're doing."

"Okay." I glance at those back hooves one more time and touch Buster's shoulder. His skin ripples a little, but he doesn't lay his ears back or act unhappy. As my hand slips below his knee—

"Oh my gosh!" I exclaim.

"I know, right? Huge difference," David says. "Dr. Mac needs to check this out."

"She's gone camping with the girls," I say, standing slowly so I don't startle Buster.

"Darn, I forgot." David stands up, too. "Do you have a cell phone on you?"

"No, but I can borrow my mom's."

"I'll stay here with these guys. Call Dr. Gabe and tell him we need him. Tell him everything you noticed about the way Buster's been acting, plus that his leg is warm, he won't let me check his shoe, and we don't see any cracks, cuts, or puncture wounds. Tell him what a rotten person Gus is, too."

"Got it!"

The size of the crowd in the store stops me in my tracks. We've never, ever had this many customers. Dad is grinning as he rings people up at the register. He winks at me as I walk by, but keeps talking to the man who is buying a post hole digger. Mom stands in the middle of the spring plants display, listening to a couple busy loading up a box with blue-and-white pansies. By the time I make it over there, the couple have gotten in line to pay for their flowers.

"There you are!" Mom has dirt on her forehead and nose, and her cheeks are red from heat or excitement, or a little of both. She looks happier than she's been since we moved here.

"How are the ponies?" she asks.

"Ah . . ." I don't want to worry her with all these customers around. "Great. We just finished."

She smiles. "I was skeptical, but you and Jules were right: the ponies were a big draw today."

I force a smile because I know she expects it. I'm super-glad business has been good, but I feel awful about Buster. "Can I use your cell? David has to call home."

"Sorry, kiddo, it's dead," she says. "I forgot to charge it again."

A tall woman with a long white braid walks up to us carrying two kinds of poison ivy killer. "Excuse me," she says to my mother.

"It's okay," I assure her. "We'll use the upstairs phone."

I take the stairs up to our apartment two at a time. Thankfully, Sophie and Jules are giggling in their bedroom. I use the kitchen phone and open the window so I can see and hear what's going on in the back lot.

Darn it! Gus has returned and is hollering at David, who is slowly walking the ponies from the grassy area to the parking lot.

Dr. Gabe picks up on the third ring. I explain everything about Buster as fast as I can. "Do you think it's serious?' I ask.

He chuckles. "I'm not that good, Josh. I actually need to see a patient before I can make a diagnosis. Ponies can go lame for lots of reasons. His shoe could be loose or, given what you told me about his owner, he's had those shoes too long. More serious issues would be laminitis, an abscess, a torn ligament or tendon, or even some kind of fracture."

"A fracture! You mean he's walking around on a broken leg?"

"I was just listing possibilities," Dr. Gabe says. "Most likely he slipped or took a funny step, kind of like the way you can twist your ankle playing soccer. If that's the case, all he needs is some rest."

Out in the parking lot, Gus stomps his foot, his face beet-red. He loses his balance a little and takes a couple steps to the side before he catches himself and starts yelling again. David is still letting Buster set the pace. They're moving at snail speed.

"Dr. Gabe, can you take a look at Buster when you get back tonight?" I ask.

"Sure, as long as the owner agrees. I should be in Ambler by five."

"Hang on." I open the window. "Hey, Gus," I shout. "Up here!"

The pony handler looks around blindly for a moment, and then he squints up at me.

"What do you want?"

"You see how Buster is limping? I've got a vet on the phone. He'll be here by five to check him out."

"What?" Gus snatches the hat off his head and throws it to the ground. "No vet's gonna steal my money, no sir-eee. Ain't happening."

David and the ponies are getting closer to the man. "His leg is really inflamed," David explains.

"No vet," Gus repeats loudly. "Get those ponies in my trailer."

I close the window so I don't have to hear Gus yell. "He said no," I tell Dr. Gabe.

"I heard," Dr. Gabe says. "I'm really sorry, Josh, but I can't treat any animal if its owner doesn't want me to."

"But he's neglecting them," I say.

"You told me that the ponies gave rides for hours; if they were truly neglected and sick, they couldn't have done that. Yes, Buster is a little lame, but we don't know why."

"They flinch when he yells at them," I say. "He doesn't groom them, and their trailer is disgusting. David thinks they might not be getting enough food."

"He doesn't sound very responsible, but neglect is usually a lot worse than what you're describing, sad to say. Tell Gus to soak Buster's foot in a warm Epsom salt bath a couple of times a day. That will help the pain and inflammation. How long is he going to be there?"

Gus opens the back gate of the horse trailer and lets the ramp drop with a crash. "Looks like he's in a hurry to leave," I say.

"I'll swing by tonight, just in case. Maybe if I talk to him face-to-face—"

I drop the phone.

Gus is trying to pull the ponies' leads out of David's hands! Babe's ears are back, and she's whinnying and tossing her head. Buster has raised his sore foot and dropped his head as low as he can. David's holding on to the leads tight, but Gus is twice his size and made of nasty. David digs his heels in and wraps the leads around his hands again, but he looks as if he doesn't know what to do next.

I do.

I fly down the stairs, shouting as loudly as I can. "Dad!"

Chapter Eight

Let them go!" I shout at Gus.

"Whadder you talking about?" Gus says. His voice sounds funny. "These are my ponies. Mine."

"I think he's drunk," David says.

"What's going on here?" shouts a loud, sharp, drill sergeant voice.

Everyone jumps—even me, and I was the one who asked for his help.

Dad rushes across the parking lot, quickly taking in the scene. "Let go of those ropes!" he orders Gus. "You're hurting David and the ponies."

"What are you gonna do if I don't?" Gus sneers.

Dad takes a long, slow breath, puts his hand on Gus's shoulder, leans forward, and whispers something to Gus. The pony handler's eyes go wide, either from the pain of Dad squeezing his shoulder, or whatever promise my father just made. Dad steps back, and Gus releases the pony leads.

"That's better," Dad says. His voice is friendly now, but his eyes are as intense as lasers. "You okay, David?"

David is rubbing the angry red marks left on his hands by tight lead ropes, but he says, "Yes, sir, thank you."

Dad points at Gus. "You've been drinking."

"Just had a couple beers," Gus protests.

"It was more than that," Dad says. "If you get behind the wheel, I'll have you arrested for driving under the influence. Now get off of my property and don't come back until you're in better shape."

Gus scowls, but he's smart enough to keep his mouth shut and leave. As soon as he disappears around the side of the building, both ponies relax. Babe nuzzles against Buster and rubs her head on his neck, nickering softly.

I laugh out loud. "That was awesome, Dad!"

"You like that?" He cracks a smile. "When you came down the stairs hollering at the top of your lungs, I wasn't quite sure what you wanted."

"Is everything okay out there?" Mom calls from the back door.

"We're fine," Dad answers. "I'll be right in." He turns to me. "Can you give me the short version of what's going on?"

David tells most of the story, and I fill in the rest, ending with Dr. Gabe's advice about soaking Buster's leg, and his promise to stop by to check on the pony around dinnertime.

"We sell Epsom salts in the store," Dad says. "Why don't you grab a box of it and a bucket? Poor little guy looks like he needs all the help he can get."

"They're hungry, too," David points out. "We gave them some hay and alfalfa pellets a couple hours ago, but . . ."

Dad tilts his head to the side. "Am I correct in guessing that the food came from the store, too?"

"Yes, sir," I admit nervously. "And the two buckets we used for their water."

Dad nodded. "Anything else?"

"Ah, yeah," I admit. "Babe, the healthy one, she ate most of the flowers and herbs Mom put in the planters yesterday."

"All of the plants," David corrects.

"All of them?" Dad asks.

I nod my head, miserable and sure I'm about to be grounded for the rest of my life.

Dad smiles, then chuckles. "This pony ate your mother's flowers. Right there on Main Street." He chuckles again, harder. "Where the entire world could watch!" He bursts into laughter. "No wonder business has been so good today—you've been entertaining the entire town." He laughs long and hard, tries to say something else, then cracks up some more.

David looks at my dad, his eyes wide and eyebrows raised. I shrug; I don't know what's going on, either.

Finally, Dad says, "Wooh!" and wipes a tear out of the corner of your eye. "Thanks, boys, I needed that. Although I'd love to see your mom's face if we showed her the planters, let's not tell her about it yet, okay?"

"Are you giving me permission to lie?" I ask.

"No," Dad says. "I'm asking you to help keep peace in the house until I figure this one out." He ruffles my hair. "Quite a day, huh? I better get inside. I'll leave the back door open. If Gus turns up again, you come and get me right away. It doesn't matter if the president himself is in the checkout line. Promise me?"

"Yes, sir," I say.

"Okay. Come with me, David," Dad says. "I'll show you where the Epsom salts are."

It takes us three tries.

The first time, we fill the bucket with warm

water, add the Epsom salts, and then try to convince Buster to put his sore foot in the bucket. He uses his good foot to kick the bucket halfway across the parking lot, soaking me for the second time that day.

When David stops laughing, he convinces Buster to put the sore foot in an empty bucket, and then he fills it with warm water. But he adds the water too quickly, and Buster shies away, kicks the bucket, and soaks David.

After we both stop laughing, I fetch more Epsom salts, alfalfa pellets, and carrots from the store (pausing to thank my father 10 million times), and we finally get it right. We move a few sections of the corral into the shade where it's cooler and tie Babe close to Buster, because having her near calms him down. While I feed them, David convinces Buster to put his bad foot in the empty bucket again. Then we slowly, very slowly, pour the warm water and Epsom salts in the bucket.

Victory!

"That's it, there you go," David soothes.

I scratch Babe's back right at the bottom of her neck, and she closes her eyes in enjoyment.

It's cool in the shadows, but the heat of the day is still coming off the blacktop, making the temperature perfect. Both horses look like they're dozing. Even David is quiet, absently patting Buster's side and keeping an eye on his sore leg. After such an insanely busy day, this is a welcome break.

"Do you think Gus really cares about these guys?" I ask.

"Not at all," David says.

"What if we could find a better place for them, maybe find someone who could buy them from Gus and give them a better life?"

"In a perfect world, right?" His voice is bitter, which surprises me.

"What about Quinn's stables? The owner is a friend of your dad, right? He must have a ton of money and plenty of space."

"He doesn't have either," David says. "He puts all of his profits back into the stables: upgrading the barn, fencing, all kinds of things. Most of the horses there are boarders; their owners pay to have Mr. Quinn take care of them. Some of the owners are months behind on their payments because of the stupid economy. Mr. Quinn can't take any charity cases, and even if he could, he doesn't have the room."

"But—"

Before I can get the next question out, Gus comes around the corner, this time with reinforcements.

Chapter Nine

Here comes trouble," I mutter.

David stands up next to me, with the horses between us. The man walking next to Gus looks to be in his sixties or so—the same age as Gus—but his eyes are clear and his face clean-shaven, and his clothes aren't all rumpled like he slept in them. The expression on his face isn't angry like Gus's, but he doesn't look like the kind of guy who's going to pay attention to what a couple of seventh graders have to say.

"I think you should get your dad," David says quietly.

"Yeah," I answer, but to my surprise, Dad is already walking our way.

"Are those the ponies you were talking about?" the new guy asks Gus.

"Hold it right there!" my father calls. "Who are you?" he asks the new guy.

"Name's Karl." The new guy reaches out to shake my father's hand. "Fellow here is paying me to drive him and his animals back to their camp. Seems like he's had a few beers and he wants to do the responsible thing. Now me, all I drink is coffee. Two spoons of sugar and a little milk."

"Responsible?" I say. "Him?"

David points to Buster. "This pony needs to see a vet."

"That's not my business," Karl says. "I'm just lending a hand. Seems—"

Gus cuts him off. "Stop yapping and load them up."

Buster whinnies nervously, and Babe tosses her head. Just being around Gus upsets them. I know how they feel; he bothers me, too.

"Just here to do a job, folks," Karl says. "Pardon me."

At least Karl knows what he's doing. He gets Babe in the trailer in a flash and doesn't rush Buster up the ramp. Before I know it, they're both in, and Karl is locking up the back gate, David at his side explaining about Buster's sore foot, and the need to soak it with Epsom salts and keep it clean.

Gus looks at my father. "You owe me for today."

Dad's gaze is steady, his eyes narrow. "You'll get paid this time tomorrow, provided you bring the ponies back and do what we agreed to. The corral stays here. I'll chain it up to make sure it doesn't get stolen."

"Sounds to me like you're the one stealing it."

"On the contrary," Dad says. "You showed up late, you let these boys do the real work, and one of your animals is lame. You better be here right on time tomorrow—with working animals and a better attitude—if you want to get paid."

Karl climbs in the cab and starts the truck, and David joins Dad and me. Gus looks like he wants to argue, but the look on my dad's face convinces him that would be a bad idea.

"We're not gonna make it to the campground unless you have money for gas," Karl calls through the open window.

"I got it," Gus snaps as he gets into the passenger seat. "We'll be back tomorrow," he says to Dad as Karl shifts the pickup into gear. "Make sure that corral don't walk away."

"Remember to soak Buster's leg," I shout as the truck pulls the trailer away.

"Remember to feed your ponies," David adds. "They're hungry!"

And then they're gone.

"Well," Dad says, reaching up to rub the back of his neck, "never thought that owning a hardware store would lead to situations like this."

"You rocked, Mr. Darrow," David says.

Dad smiles. "At least we kept a drunk driver off the road."

I know how important that is, but it's hard to be too enthusiastic, knowing that Buster and Babe are stuck with an owner who doesn't care about them and that Buster is injured.

"Why did you make such a big deal about the corral?" I ask. "Aren't the ponies more important?"

"Of course they are," Dad says. "I was just trying to find a way to make sure he'll show up again. Gus seems to be motivated by money and nothing else."

Mom appears at the back door. "Honey, I could use some help. And David? Your mom just called and asked me to send you home." She disappears back inside without waiting for an answer.

"Gotta go, boys," Dad says.

I look at David. "I thought your dad was going to pick you up," I say.

"I thought so, too," David says, his eyes clouded.

"Well, sorry I can't stick around to help you clean up, Josh. I'll call you tomorrow night, okay?"

"What about Dr. Gabe?" I ask.

"Just call him," David says. "Tell him what we did and what happened. Maybe he'll have some advice about tomorrow."

After David leaves, I shovel the pony dung to the far corner of the lot, then sweep up the trash and Gus's cigarette butts and throw them into the Dumpster. With each push of the broom, I get angrier about Gus, more worried about Babe and Buster, and more frustrated that I can't figure out how to save them.

Once the parking lot is tidy I help Jules restock the shelves and displays in the store. Looks like everyone in Ambler—heck, everyone in the whole county—bought something at Wrenches & Roses today. Even my hammer display has to be restocked. Mom and Dad are both beaming and talking about how their hard work might be paying off.

It should be a perfect family evening, especially when my parents decide to celebrate a great day by splurging on pizza for dinner. But I can't shake my dark mood. I'm not really old enough to make a difference, like the way Dad got rid of Gus earlier.

And I'm too old to be innocent the way Sophie is, drawing pictures and singing her pony song without realizing that Buster and Babe work for a man who might turn them into dog meat one of these days.

I'm so blue I can't even finish my pizza.

When I ask to be excused, my parents look puzzled but give me permission. I drag myself down the hall and flop face-first on my bed.

Two minutes later Jules pounds on my door.

"Get up! Sunita called—we have to go to the clinic right away. It's an emergency!"

Chapter Ten

As we jog down Main Street, Jules fills me in.

"It's Ranger," she says.

"Another porcupine?" I ask, horrified.

"I don't think so, but Sunita said it's life-threatening. Mr. Fedor is bringing him to the clinic right now. Dr. Gabe just got off the turnpike."

"What about David or Brenna? They should be there; they've seen way more of this stuff than we have."

"Sunita didn't say, she just told us to hurry."

When we arrive, Sunita is unlocking the clinic's front door, and Mr. Fedor is struggling to lift Ranger—his eighty-pound mutt—out of the backseat of his car.

"Mr. Fedor," Jules starts.

"We can help you," I finish.

With the door now wide open, Sunita runs back to lend a hand. We each grab an edge of Ranger's blanket and together we all carry the big dog inside.

"He didn't eat much yesterday," Mr. Fedor says. "I thought his mouth was sore from the porcupine quills. He wouldn't eat this morning and slept most of the day, but that made sense to me because of the painkillers." He pauses as we maneuver through the door and into the clinic's waiting room.

"Dolittle Room," Sunita says quietly.

Mr. Fedor continues his story as we make our way down the hall. "Then this afternoon he vomited and had diarrhea. Now he can't even walk."

We make our way into the examination room.

"On three, ready?" Sunita asks. "One, two . . . three."

We lift the dog onto the stainless steel table. Ranger whimpers, and Mr. Fedor's eyes fill with tears. Jules shoots me a look over the dog's stretched-out body. Ranger is panting, but he's lying totally still. Not a good sign.

Sunita disappears for an instant and returns with Ranger's file, a clipboard, and a pen. She's the cat expert of the Vet Volunteers, but she can deal with pretty much anything.

"Dr. Gabe should be here any second," she says to Mr. Fedor. "If you can answer a few questions for me, he'll be able to take care of Ranger even faster when he gets here. When was the last time he drank anything?"

Mr. Fedor frowns and keeps stroking Ranger's silky head. "He's had water a couple times today. The last time must have been a little after two, when I came in from mowing the lawn."

Sunita makes a note. "When was the last time he ate?"

"Yesterday, just before dinner, maybe four thirty," he says. "I soaked his dog food in water and a little beef broth."

"Nothing at all since then?" Sunita asks. "No treats? No leftovers?"

He looks up. "Do leashes count?"

"Excuse me?" Sunita asks.

"I don't know when he did it." Mr. Fedor pulls a well-chewed strand of leather out of his pocket. "Could have been last week for all I know, but I found this under the kitchen table this afternoon. It's missing at least a foot, plus the metal chain."

Somehow Sunita keeps her feelings off her face. "The more information we have the better," she says.

"You don't think it's inside him, do you?" Jules asks.

"Dr. Mac has told a lot of stories about the strange things that pets eat," Sunita says. "Sometimes it passes right through them, and sometimes it requires surgery. My cat Mittens ate some yarn once, and Dr. Mac had to operate to remove it. But don't worry," she quickly adds, "Mittens came through the surgery and was her old self in days."

The bell on the front door jingles, and an instant later, Dr. Gabe rushes into the room. "Hello, hello," he says pleasantly. "I see our good friend Ranger is back for a return engagement."

He quickly takes Ranger's vital signs—his temperature, pulse, and rate of breathing. Sunita writes all the numbers down and repeats Mr. Fedor's information as Dr. Gabe feels Ranger's belly and checks his gums. Ranger whimpers but is so lethargic he doesn't struggle or squirm.

"Is he going to be okay?" Mr. Fedor asks anxiously.

Dr. Gabe steps over to the sink, rolls up his sleeves, and starts scrubbing his hands with antiseptic soap and a brush. "He's a little dehydrated, and he's in shock. First thing is to get some fluids into him; then I'll X-ray his stomach and digestive tract. That should show us what we're dealing with. Jules, will you please take Mr. Fedor into the waiting room?"

"I'd rather stay with Ranger," Mr. Fedor says. "I can help keep him calm."

"I know you can," Dr. Gabe says kindly. "It's obvious how much you two love each other. But there's a small chance I might need to operate quickly. The best thing you can do for Ranger is to hold him in your heart and wait for him out there."

He glances at Jules, and she springs into action.

"Come on, Mr. Fedor." She lightly touches his elbow. "I'll show you the most comfortable chair. Can I make you some tea?"

Mr. Fedor looks forlornly at Ranger. "Bye, buddy," he says as he leans in to kiss the dog's head. "I'll see you soon."

Ranger's tail thumps weakly on the table. Mr. Fedor sniffs loudly and follows my sister out the door.

"Sunita, I need an IV bag." Dr. Gabe is already shaving a patch of fur off Ranger's foreleg. "Do you want to stay for this, Josh?"

I nod before I think too much about what he's saying.

Dr. Gabe rubs antiseptic on the shaved patch of leg. "Scrub up."

Sunita joins me at the sink after she hands Dr. Gabe the IV solution, both of us watching him over our shoulders as we scrub our hands with stiff brushes. He inserts a needle into Ranger's leg and gets the IV fluid flowing before I remember that needles make me queasy. There's no time for that today.

"This will hydrate Ranger and, I hope, stabilize him a bit," Dr. Gabe explains. He unlocks a cabinet and fills two syringes from bottles inside it, then injects the fluid in the syringes into the IV line. "This first one is a sedative and the other is an antibiotic, because this big guy is fighting one heck of an infection."

He flicks the brakes off the wheels of the exam table with the toe of his shoe. "I'm going to run him down for X-rays. You two stay here until I call."

"Are you sure you don't need help holding him down?" Sunita inquires.

Dr. Gabe looks grim. "No, he's just lost consciousness, so I can handle it on my own."

He's halfway down the hall before I can speak.

"Does he always move that fast?" I ask.

"Only in emergencies," Sunita says with a serious face.

"What happens next?"

"It depends on what the X-ray shows. If Ranger really ate that leash, Dr. Gabe will have to open him up to get it out of there."

My stomach flops. "Surgery?"

"It's the only way in a case like this."

"I'm not really a Vet Volunteer, you know. I don't know what to do."

"It's okay, Josh," Sunita says with a kind smile. "Dr. Gabe's the one who went to four years of college and six years of vet school. I'm allowed to hand him instruments, but that's because I've seen a lot of this, plus my parents are doctors. If you want to watch because you're interested, you can. If you don't want to watch, you don't have to. No pressure either way."

The intercom crackles. "You guys want to see these films?" Dr. Gabe asks.

In just a few minutes, Dr. Gabe has the X-rays mounted on a light board. It's easy to see the outlines of Ranger's spine, ribs, and hips. Dr. Gabe points to the glowing white links of the metal collar he swallowed and the dark, snakelike shadow that is the leash.

"Isn't it a little weird for a dog to eat something like that?" I ask.

"Not at all. I know vets who have removed dentures, spoons, toy dinosaurs . . . you name it, some dog somewhere has swallowed it." He flicks on the overhead lights. "The good news is that Ranger is young and strong. It doesn't look as if the leash and chain damaged his esophagus or stomach, and Mr. Fedor brought him here before the leash moved on too far. The bad news is that I have to remove the leash before it causes more damage. Something like this can absolutely kill a dog."

We follow him as he wheels Ranger to the operating room. "I assume you'll lend a hand, Sunita," Dr. Gabe says. "Do you want to watch, Josh?"

I've seen Dr. Mac and Dr. Gabe examine lots of pets in the past couple of months. I've even watched them stitch up a few. And of course I've helped take care of loads of animals postsurgery. But I've never actually seen surgery itself. To be honest, I'm not sure that I want to, but my mouth opens up and somehow I say, "Sure. That would be great."

Everything happens very, very fast.

We put on shoe coverings and surgical scrubs over our clothes, then we scrub our hands again and put on latex gloves and face masks, all to reduce the chance of exposing Ranger to germs. Dr. Gabe gets a surgical tray and a sterilized surgical kit ready.

"Will you be using an endoscope?" Sunita asks.

"What's that?" I ask.

"It's a thin tube with a camera on the end," Dr. Gabe explains. "It's inserted into the patient's mouth and down the esophagus so we can see whatever the animal swallowed and remove it. But what Ranger has in his belly is too big to be removed with an endoscope. Surgery is his best bet."

Dr. Gabe asks me to move a light so he can see better, then he intubates Ranger by inserting a tube down his esophagus. Sunita helps by holding Ranger's mouth open. "Ranger will get oxygen and anesthesia through this tube," Dr. Gabe says. "And now I'll connect this plastic clip to his tongue. See? It has a light sensor to monitor his oxygen and blood. These other small clips connect to the pulse oximeter. That's a monitoring machine we use to track his pulse rate." Dr. Gabe checks the readings that are shown on the screen next to the operating table, then he shaves Ranger's belly and applies a sterile cloth with a portion cut out where he intends to operate. I move around a couple of times, trying to find a place to stand where I won't be in the way but where I have a clear view of what's going on. It's hard to believe that an hour ago I was sitting at our kitchen table eating a slice of double-pepperoni, double-cheese pizza.

Sunita hands the doctor a bottle of antiseptic that he uses to clean and sterilize the bare skin of Ranger's abdomen. Then he picks up a scalpel, a knife with a shiny blade that flashes in the bright overhead light, and it suddenly hits me what I'm about to see.

My stomach flops and flops again. I break out in a cold sweat, and my ears start ringing. I get a funny taste in my mouth, and it feels like the floor is moving a little.

Dr. Gabe looks at me over the top of his mask. "Josh? You feel okay?"

"Uh-oh." Sunita grabs my arm. "You don't look so good."

"I don't feel too good, either," I admit.

"No worries," Dr. Gabe says. "Happens to everyone. But Dr. Mac has a rule—no puking in the operating room. Ever. You cool with that?"

I try to nod, but it makes me feel dizzier.

"Take him out, Sunita. Get his head low and feet high."

Sunita puts her arm around me and helps me to the door.

"Sorry," I croak.

"Don't worry about it, Josh," Dr. Gabe says. "We'll talk later."

Chapter Eleven

I stumble out the door and let Sunita guide me to the bathroom, but I won't let her take me in.

"No," I say firmly. "I'm just a little queasy. I can manage the bathroom on my own."

"But what if you pass out?" she asks. "What if your blood pressure goes so low you forget to breathe? What if you hit your head on the corner of the sink and it gives you amnesia and you wake up not even knowing your own name? Or you could get retrograde amnesia, though I'm not sure what that means, exactly."

"I'm fine," I say, trying to cover my embarrassment. "But you could get me something to drink, if you want."

"Good idea. There's always juice in Dr. Mac's fridge. Orange, apple, carrot, mango? She probably has chocolate milk, too. Did you eat dinner? Low blood sugar can bring on fainting episodes and nausea, too. Maybe you should have a snack that combines proteins and carbs, like cheese and an apple. Does that sound good?"

Sunita is usually the quietest Vet Volunteer, so I'm confused by all this chattering until her strategy dawns on me.

"I get it," I say with a smile. "You're just trying to distract me, aren't you? That's the reason for all this gobbledygook about amnesia and cheese."

She smiles, too. "You figured out my plan."

Along with being the quietest Vet Volunteer, I think she's the prettiest, which is another reason I want to die of embarrassment about what just happened in the operating room.

"And it wasn't gobbledygook," she insists. "Based on the fact that you don't look pale and clammy anymore, I'd say I achieved my goal."

Pale and clammy? Great.

"Well, thanks," I say. "But I need some time alone in here, if you know what I mean."

"Oh," she blushes. "Right. Sure. I'll put your snack in the waiting room."

"No, don't," I say. "You should be helping in

the operating room. If I don't faint, hit my head, and forget my name, I'll ask Jules to get me some milk."

"Okay," she says.

"Okay," I say. "Bye." I close the door and lean my forehead against it. *Pale and clammy?* As if this day couldn't get any worse.

I splash cold water on my face and wash my hands. Embarrassing myself in front of Sunita and Dr. Gabe was bad enough, but what if it means that I don't have what it takes to be a vet? Veterinarians have to be tough. They have to perform under pressure. They can't get woozy and throw up at the sight of blood, and especially not *before* the sight of blood.

I stare at my reflection in the mirror. "Sometimes you can be a real idiot."

I slump down next to my sister in the waiting room, lean forward, and put my head in my hands.

"What happened?" Jules asks. "Is Ranger okay? You look terrible."

"Ranger's on the operating table," I say. "Sunita's helping Dr. Gabe. I hate myself, and I'm never going to be a vet."

"What? What do you mean? Sit up, you're not making any sense."

I sit up, lean my head against the wall, and tell her what happened.

"Dr. Mac doesn't allow anyone to puke in the operating room," Jules says seriously.

"I know! You're not making me feel any better."

"Stop it." She gives me a friendly shove. "Everybody feels like that the first time. I had a long talk with Dr. Mac about it a few days after she stitched up Cuddles."

"Really?"

She nods. "She said I shouldn't be embarrassed: medical things can be intense, and it takes time to get used to them. When do you think Ranger will be out of the OR?"

"No idea," I say. "Where's Mr. Fedor?"

"He's pacing up and down the driveway, talking to his son in Florida. Did you know that he's a retired dairy farmer? He's the sweetest old guy, ever."

"A farmer?" I sit up straight. "Does he still have pasture land? Do you think he'd adopt two ponies? They'd be great companions for Ranger."

"He sold the farm when his wife got sick," Jules says. "It sounds like Ranger is all he really has left."

The door opens, but instead of Mr. Fedor, it's Brenna who walks in. "David texted me that you guys were here," she says. "Is it Ranger?"

My sister brings her up to date on the mutt's latest adventure, tactfully leaving out the part where I was ejected from the operating room.

"No wonder Mr. Fedor looks so sad," she says.

"Did David tell you about Buster's bad leg?" I ask.

"No." She sits cross-legged on the chair across from us and listens as I explain everything we did for Buster and how Gus reacted.

"Are you kidding me?" Brenna throws her hands in the air. "Why didn't you call me?"

"What could you have done? Dr. Gabe said that he couldn't treat an animal without the owner's permission."

"But if Buster doesn't get treated, that's abuse," Brenna says.

"But that hasn't exactly happened yet," Jules points out.

"If Buster is worse tomorrow and Gus still won't let a vet treat him, we could call Animal Control, right?" I ask.

"Absolutely." Brenna's nose scrunches up. "But Mr. Snyder, the local guy, is on a fishing trip with my dad. They went way into the mountains, out of cell-phone range."

"Wouldn't he have a backup, the way that Dr. Gabe is covering for Dr. Mac this weekend?"

"The state doesn't have enough money for that," Brenna says. "We'll have to wait for Mr. Snyder to come back."

"I'm tired of waiting," I say angrily. "I want to help Buster right now. Tonight."

"Okay, let's get positive and practical," Jules says. "If Mr. Snyder gets back in time and says that Gus isn't taking good care of Buster, what would happen?"

"That's tough." Brenna sighs. "He'd have to find a place for the pony, probably with the help of a pony- or horse-rescue group. I remember my mom talking about a retirement ranch for horses once, but I think that's in Arizona. It could take weeks or longer to find him a new home."

"Could he stay at your house until a permanent place is found?" I ask.

Brenna shakes her head sadly. "Our barn is already filled with rescue critters. Mom had to send an injured hawk across the state to a rehab center that had room."

"David's going to the horse show with his father tomorrow," I say. "They could ask around there, find a local place that can help."

"His dad promised to take him to the horse show?" Brenna asks.

"Yeah, he was really excited about it," I say. "He

spent half the day bragging about how incredible his dad is with horses."

Brenna frowns. "Well, Mr. Hutchinson might be good with horses, but he's terrible with his kids. He's always making big promises to David, and he never follows through."

Jules and I exchange glances. Our father doesn't make much money, but we can always count on him to tell us the truth, and to be there when we really need him.

"That's why we all cut David a little slack," Brenna adds. "He can be a little annoying sometimes, but he has a heart of gold. Let's get back to Buster. Which one of you is better at researching on the Internet?"

We're both pretty good, so we decide who gets to use the clinic's computer with the traditional Vet Volunteers method: a quick game of rock paper scissors. Jules shoots scissors, I shoot rock, and I get to spend the next half hour in charge of the keyboard and mouse with the girls watching and commenting over my shoulders. By the time Mr. Fedor steps in, we've started a list of rescue societies to contact, even though they are all at least a thousand miles away from Ambler.

"Any news?" Mr. Fedor asks.

"I'll go back and ask for an update," Brenna says.

"How about that cup of tea now?" Jules asks.

"That would be nice," Mr. Fedor says as he lowers himself into a chair. "You kids are sweet to take such good care of an old guy like me."

"I haven't been here that long, sir," I say, "but it seems that people who care about animals are pretty good at caring about people, too."

He nods, twisting the gold wedding band on his left hand. "Sounds like something my wife would say. She died last year, you know."

"No, sir, I didn't know that. I'm very sorry."

He nods absently. "After Nora passed, my son made me go out and get a dog. Thought I needed companionship. Crazy dog chewed up every shoe I owned, but I couldn't help myself; I fell in love with the fool thing. Don't want to think about how I'd get along without him."

"Then don't," I say firmly. "Dr. Gabe is a great doctor, and Ranger is strong and stubborn. Everything is going to be fine."

The door at the end of the hall opens and Dr. Gabe walks briskly toward us, followed by Brenna.

"Ranger is a trouper," Dr. Gabe announces with a big smile on his face. "I think the worst is behind him."

Mr. Fedor grabs Dr. Gabe's hand and pumps it

up and down. "Thank you, young man, thank you!" He beams.

"It was quite the gastrointestinal blockage," Dr. Gabe explains. "I removed not only the portion of leash and chain that you suspected, but also what looks like some carpet fibers and a plastic bottle cap!"

"Really?" Mr. Fedor asks, dumbfounded.

"Really. But we got his digestive tract cleared, and he's stable now. He's all stitched up, resting comfortably in the recovery room. You can see him soon, but we'll need to keep him here overnight for observation."

Mr. Fedor almost looks like he's going to cry with happiness. "I can't thank you enough," he says as he vigorously shakes Dr. Gabe's hand again. Then Mr. Fedor turns to me and shakes my hand, too, and then Brenna's, like he doesn't know what to do with all the joy he's feeling.

While Dr. Gabe continues to talk to Mr. Fedor about Ranger's recovery, Jules, Brenna, and I help Sunita clean up the operating room. Dr. Mac always tells us that keeping things clean and sterile is the first line of defense for good care in any veterinary clinic. Sunita gives us the details of the operation while we scrub.

"Guys, you should have seen it. He knew exactly where to make the incision to reach the stomach. Then he had to find the blockage, remove it, and stitch Ranger up again. Some of the blockage was in Ranger's stomach and some had started to move to his intestine, so Dr. Gabe got in there just in time. Ugh, it was gross but really fascinating."

"Don't you ever feel queasy watching the surgeries?" Jules asks her.

"Oh sure, of course. Especially my first few times seeing people's pets injured or being operated on. But now I just focus on thinking positive. I concentrate on how we are helping the animals in the long run. Plus, when Dr. Gabe and Dr. Mac administer sedatives, I know the animals aren't feeling any pain."

After Mr. Fedor leaves, Dr. Gabe thanks us for helping out and tells us he'll be staying overnight on Dr. Mac's couch to monitor Ranger. He says good-bye to the girls and asks me to stay for a minute.

My stomach flops again, but I stay. As the door closes behind my sister, I say, "I know I screwed up, but please don't hold that against Buster."

"Buster?" he asks.

"The lame pony," I remind him. "Could you come and check him tomorrow, please?"

"Of course," Dr. Gabe says. "Now, about that little episode in the operating room."

"Yeah," I mutter, embarrassed. Dr. Gabe will probably never invite me to observe any of his surgeries again. "I'm really sorry about that."

"There's nothing to be sorry about, dude. It happens. Next time, breathe in and out through your mouth, slow and steady, to keep your blood oxygenated. I had to do it a lot when I was starting out."

"And you got over it?" I ask.

"I did," Dr. Gabe says. "It should be better the next time."

Next time. Dr. Gabe said, *Next time.* And that gives me hope.

Chapter Twelve

When we get home, Mom and Dad are curled up on the couch reading a book to Sophie.

"Is everything okay?" Mom asks.

"Dr. Gabe saved the day," Jules says. "Josh got to see how he prepped Ranger for surgery. He saw the X-rays, too."

I wait, but she doesn't tell them about the humiliating part of the night. As far as sisters go, Jules can be the best, if she's in the right mood.

"Not the way I'd want to spend a Saturday night," Mom comments.

"It was pretty cool," I say. "The best part was the look on Mr. Fedor's face when Dr. Gabe told him Ranger would be okay."

"We're reading about ponies, Josh!" Sophie announces.

"Speaking of that," I say carefully, "how do you think tomorrow is going to go? I mean, do you think the, um, outside entertainment will show up?" I'm trying to ask the question in a way that won't upset Sophie.

"I've been thinking about that," Mom says. "It wouldn't hurt to have a backup plan ready. Maybe a repeat of this morning?"

"Can we do it when we wake up?" Jules whines. "I'm sooooo tired."

"I'll do it," I offer.

Everyone stares at me, shocked that I'm volunteering for extra work in the store.

"I'm not tired," I explain. "The last thing I want to do is sit around in my room."

"Well, okay then," Dad says. "Get to it!"

After I set up the rabbitat, I clean up and organize the small area where little kids could draw. Mom is pretty good at face painting; the store was too busy today, but if it's slower tomorrow, she might want to offer her services, so I rummage in the storeroom until I unearth all of the face-painting supplies. I clean them up and lay them on a shelf behind the register, along with paper towels and sponges. The last thing I do is sweep the aisles and empty the trash cans into the Dumpster.

The wind has picked up since the afternoon, but it's a strange warm wind, blowing from the south. It rustles the trees and my hair and hurries the clouds over the face of the fat moon. The wind makes me restless, frustrated, confused about almost everything. And worried.

How does Buster feel? Did Gus let them out of the trailer? Did he even give them water or hay? What if he decides that the corral panels aren't worth coming back for? Maybe he stole them in the first place. What if he decides that Buster is too much trouble? What if he abandons the pony at the side of the road . . . or worse?

A sharp burst of wind rakes through the parking lot, causing the corral panels to fall with a loud clatter. The trees bow and sway, scattering blossoms and new leaves.

I want to . . .

I can't . . .

I shouldn't. . . .

I will . . .

I have to find that campsite and save the ponies.

I can't take off until Mom and Dad are asleep, but that gives me plenty of time to get ready. The first thing is to borrow a few supplies: a gallon jug for hot water, a box of Epsom salts, and the last bag of alfalfa pellets. I'll need to take Mom's cell phone, which means I have to find it and charge it. Hmmm . . . That one's going to require some more thought.

I head down to the Vet Volunteer room in the basement to use the ancient computer. It's so slow I want to scream, but instead I practice my calm and steady deep breaths and gradually click through to a map of Ambler. I zoom out and try to figure where Gus and the ponies might be staying.

Okay, this is getting a little complicated.

Eventually, I settle on three possible sites. I print out a map and directions to all three, and try not to wince when I see how many miles I'll be biking. I put the directions and the rest of the supplies in my backpack. The last thing is to pump up the tires on my bike because my parents will definitely be sleeping with their windows open tonight, and I need to get out as quietly as possible.

I find the hand pump and a flashlight in the storage closet, head up to the store, and tiptoe across the squeaky wooden boards. Mom and Sophie are giggling upstairs with Jules. There's a baseball game on the television, so I know where Dad is, too. I sneak out the back door, walk the length of the building to our bike rack, put the flashlight in my mouth, and kneel down to unscrew the valve on the back tire of my bike.

"Kind of late for a bike ride," says a deep voice in the dark. "Don't you think?"

"Dad?" I shine the flashlight up the alley and find him standing there with a trowel in one hand and a potted begonia in the other. "What are you doing?"

"That's *my* question," he says mildly.

"My tires need air," I say, sticking to the truth.

"Is there any reason they need air right now?" he asks. "Nobody goes out on a bike ride at night—alone—right? Because that would extremely dangerous, I'm guessing."

Busted.

"I was thinking about it," I admit with a sigh. "But I was going to bring Mom's cell phone with me so I'd be safe."

"Come help me with these flowers," Dad suggests. "I did everything in my power to keep your mom from checking her planters today."

Under the faint glow from the streetlight on the corner, Dad and I plant new flowers and herbs to replace those that Babe had devoured for her breakfast. Slowly, I fill Dad in about my plans to find the campsite, take pictures of the bad conditions that Gus forces the ponies to live in, and give Buster's leg another soaking treatment.

"And you were going to do all of that at night, in the middle of nowhere, by yourself?" Dad asks.

"It sounded like a better plan when it was in my head," I admit. "Saying it out loud . . . well, it doesn't sound quite as good."

"If you were a superhero, it would be easier and safer. I'm proud of your compassion, Josh." Dad pauses to pat the soil down around the roots of a basil plant. "The world needs more kids like you and your friends, kids who understand animals and try to make their lives better." He sits on the edge of the planter. "But riding off in the darkness like that, tracking a man who could be drunk, who could be dangerous. Son, that's plain foolish. Compassion without intelligence won't get you very far."

The words sting, even though I know he's right. "But Dad, we have to do something."

He moves on to the next planter, pulls a root ball out of the dirt, and tosses it into a cardboard box. "Dr. Gabe said he'll stop by to look over the ponies, right? And Brenna, the one with the crow, she's trying to get the Animal Control fellow involved."

"Yes, but—"

"But nothing. Josh, you've done everything you can. This is in the hands of adults now, professionals, whose job it is to handle these things."

"And they're not taking it seriously. You saw Gus. He doesn't care about Babe and Buster. They make money for him, that's all."

Dad carefully lowers a zinnia plant into the dirt. "You know the worst part of being a parent?"

The question puzzles me. "Paying for sneakers every time we outgrow them?"

"No, it's having to watch your children learn that the world is not a fair place. I hate to admit it, son, but there's a good chance that you can't win this battle, no matter how stubborn you are, no matter that your heart is in the right place."

I sniff and try to swallow the lump that's stuck in my throat.

"I stubbornly disagree, Dad."

Chapter Thirteen

I wake up confused. More confused than usual. It was after two in the morning before I finally fell asleep, because—

All of the memories of yesterday crash down on me. *Buster. Babe. Gus. Dr. Gabe. Ranger.*

The clock shows nine thirty in the morning. Nine thirty!

I jump out of the bed and run downstairs, hollering, "Why didn't anybody wake me up?"

Jules and Sophie look up from the cartoons they're watching in the living room.

"Why aren't you dressed?" I ask. "We have so much to do!"

"Josh," Jules says.

I grab my head in my hands. "I can't believe Mom didn't wake me up."

"Josh!" Jules shouts. "Calm down! It's Sunday, you goof. The store doesn't open until noon, remember? We sleep in on Sunday."

"Sunday," I repeat. "Are Mom and Dad downstairs?"

"They went to Lou's for bagels. I hope they get back soon, I'm starving."

"So, I'm not late," I say.

"No, but you really stink. Take a shower, will you? Hey, where are you going?" she calls after me. "You're not supposed to wear your pajamas downstairs!"

I hurry all the way down to the basement and boot up the computer. Jules walks in as I am impatiently tapping the top of the monitor, even though I know that won't speed things up.

"What's going on?" Jules asks.

"I couldn't sleep last night," I confess. "I came down here and did some research."

"You did homework on a Saturday night?" She pretends to faint onto the couch. "What's next? A zombie invasion?"

"It wasn't homework, it was real research. It started with this." I hold up the grubby business card that I found next to the register. "His full name is Gus Blusterfeld. But it wasn't as easy as I thought it was going to be. Turns out there are a lot of Gus Blusterfelds in the world."

"I hope they're not all like the one we know."

"Me, too. It took a couple hours and a lot of mistakes, but I finally found a couple of sites that Gus was listed on—party-planning sites mostly. Get this: the listings were under two names, Gustav and Gloria Blusterfeld."

"How do you know it's the right Gus?"

"Because they all had photos of Buster and Babe."

"Is Gloria his wife?"

"I don't know. I sent e-mails to every site I found, but I haven't heard back from anyone yet. The more information we have about Gus, the better. But I can't hang out on the computer all day."

"I'll come down here and check whenever I can," Jules says.

"Thanks. Do me a favor and call Brenna, too. Ask if that Animal Control officer is back yet." My e-mail alert beeps and I click to open the new message.

"Is it about Gus?" she asks.

"No." I read and reread the message. "It's David. He's on his way over."

"I thought he was going to a horse show or something with his dad."

"Looks like his plans changed," I say.

"Ouch," Jules says.

"Yeah," I agree. "Ouch."

By the time I get out of the shower, Mom and Dad have returned, and the kitchen is filled with the smell of the best bagels in the world, toasted and smothered with cream cheese. David is here, too, working his way through a French-toast bagel. He doesn't look like he got much sleep, either.

"Hey," I say, putting the halves of my everything bagel in the toaster.

"Hey," he says.

Mom and Dad are downstairs putting the finishing touches on the store. Jules and Sophie are eating in the living room.

I watch the wires inside the toaster glow hot. David usually talks a hundred miles a minute. He's always joking, teasing, showing off to get a laugh.

My bagel halves toast in silence, then pop.

"Are you okay?" I ask.

"Yeah."

"No, you're not." I put the bagel on a plate and carry it to the table. "What's going on? Why aren't you at the horse show?"

He just gives a snort and pushes the cream cheese across the table to me.

"I spent a lot of time online last night," I say, changing the subject, "trying to learn more about Gus and find a better home for the ponies."

He doesn't respond, so I tell him everything I found. By the time I've finished the bagel, he knows everything, but I'm still puzzled.

"Did something go wrong with your dad?" I ask.

He looks up at me. "Why do you care? You have the perfect family."

"Ha!" I laugh. "Perfect? We're broke. If business doesn't pick up soon, we're going to have to move in with my grandparents. We're always arguing. Half the time Sophie thinks she's a pony or a rabbit or a raccoon. We've never been to Disneyworld, and I'm pretty sure we'll never go. My parents expect me to be exactly like Jules, only the boy version. We are a long way from perfect, trust me."

"Yeah, but your parents don't make promises and break them."

That's true.

"That's why you're not at the horse show, right?" I ask.

He nods. "He said he had to go into work. He promised he'd make it up to me." He shrugs, like he's trying not to care. "Whatever."

I can't imagine what it would feel like if that

happened to me. Looking at David, I get the sense that it happens a lot.

"That really sucks," I say.

"Yeah, it does." He stabs the cream cheese with a knife. "Don't tell the girls, okay?"

"Ok, I . . . whoops." I say.

"What?" he asks. "What's wrong?"

"I almost said 'I promise,' but then I realized that you might not like it if I said that. So . . . what I am supposed to say?"

He gives a half laugh. "You could say, 'David is the all-seeing, all-knowing horse genius and stand-up comedian who is my best friend and will save the world.'"

"No way!" I flick a spoonful of cream cheese, and it hits him square in the nose. "How about 'David is a pain in the butt, but he's my best friend and we'll save the world together.'"

He pops the cream cheese in his mouth. "Deal."

A loud horn blares in the parking lot. We both run to the window.

The ponies have arrived for Day Two.

Chapter Fourteen

By the time we get outside, Karl, the guy who drove the ponies away yesterday, is opening the trailer. Gus is nowhere in sight.

"Sorry I'm late," Karl says as he lays the end of the ramp on the ground. "Gus only called me a little while ago."

Gus obviously forgot that we didn't open until noon on Sundays. For once, his incompetence was a good thing.

"Where is Gus?" David asks.

Karl backs Babe out of the trailer. "He's not feeling so good this morning. Here, take this," Karl hands Babe's lead to David. "I'm just dropping the ponies off."

"What time will Gus get here?" I ask as he heads back into the trailer.

"He's coming to pick them up at one," Karl says.

"What! But the pony rides go until four today!"

"I dunno about that," Karl says. "Gus just said to tell you to have these critters ready by one. That's all I know."

David and I watch anxiously as Buster slowly emerges, limping much worse than he had yesterday. David opens his mouth to say something, but I put my fingers to my lips. We don't want Karl to take back any of the details of our plan to Gus.

I take Buster's lead rope. He looks up at me—his face tight with pain—sniffs my hand, and sighs heavily.

I pat his neck. "Poor guy," I say. "You had a rough night, didn't you?"

Buster swings his head toward me and lets me scratch his chin. His feet and Babe's are caked in manure. When they left last night, their hooves were much cleaner than they are now.

"Did Gus keep the ponies locked in that trailer all night?" I ask angrily. "Did he even feed them?"

Karl looks up from the trailer hitch. "Gus is paying me to drop off the ponies and bring his truck back to camp. You seem like nice kids, but honestly, that's all I know. Have a good one." He gets into the cab, waves out the window, and slowly drives away.

David is already focused on Buster. "How you feeling there, buddy?" he asks. "How's that foot?" He moves his hands from the pony's shoulder down the leg. "Definitely warmer," he says. "And more swollen."

"Stay with him," I say. "I'll get everything we need."

In just a few minutes we have our mini-triage station assembled. The problem is our patient doesn't want to cooperate.

"Come on, buddy, just pick up your foot a little bit." David pleads.

"Just an inch," I add.

"Let's try something else," David suggests.

We have Buster lift and lower his other feet, taking it slowly and loving him up, then we try to get him to lift the injured foot.

"Ready?" David asks.

I nod, poised to slip the empty bucket under the hoof when it's off the ground so we can start the treatment.

"One, two . . ."

Buster lifts the foot on "two." I get the bucket in position, but the nasty smell makes me gag. "Yuck!" I say.

David wrinkles his nose and leans away from the stink. "That's a really bad sign."

"I'll call the doc."

"Is the pony in distress, breathing hard?" Dr. Gabe asks on the other end of the phone. "Is he foaming at the mouth or unable to stand up?"

It's tempting to lie because it might get him here faster, but I make myself do the hard thing. The right thing.

"No, sir," I admit. "The leg is warmer than it was yesterday, more swollen, too." I look out the window. "Right now he's drinking water."

"Don't let anyone ride him," Dr. Gabe says.

"We won't," I promise. "But Gus is picking them up early, at one. I told you that he called them dog meat yesterday, didn't I? How soon can you be here?"

Dr. Gabe covers the phone and says "I'll be right there" to someone in the clinic. To me he says, "A two-year-old Labradoodle that was hit by a minivan was just carried in. I have to go, Josh."

David and I don't stop moving for the next hour, first setting up the riding corral, next grooming the horses. Buster stands calmly, sore leg soaking in the bucket of Epsom salts while I go over his coat with the currycomb and the brush. David does the same with Babe; then he takes out the tools to check her hooves.

"I still feel rotten I didn't do this yesterday," he says, picking up Babe's foot.

"You're doing it today," I point out. "That's what matters."

"No." David shakes his head. "You're doing it."

"What?"

"Time for your next lesson in horse maintenance. Come here."

David shows me how to check and clean each of Babe's hooves with a hoof pick that has a small brush attached to one side. It's a little scary at first, especially when I pick up Babe's first front foot. But I do what David says, first running my hand down Babe's front leg and giving a bit of a squeeze near the bottom so she will pick up her foot.

I'm not queasy, not yet, but I sure am nervous. I take a deep breath, and another, slower than the first. David talks to both Babe and me in a quiet, low voice. I work carefully and steadily and keep breathing. Babe stands there patiently. After I pick and brush out that first front hoof, David shows me how to run my hand along her side and down her back leg so she knows which foot I'm headed for next.

I finish cleaning that back hoof then move on to

check her other front hoof. I run my hand down her leg and squeeze; she lifts the foot, almost like magic. Babe's last hoof has a small stone stuck next to the frog, the bottom part of the hoof that acts like a shock absorber.

"What should I do about that?" I ask.

"Try getting it out with your finger or the brush," David advises. "You don't want to pick too hard at the frog; it's really sensitive. You only use a pick there as a last resort."

"Okay," I say. But I hesitate.

"Go ahead," David encourages me. "You can do it."

I take another breath and dig my finger in and—the stone comes out! I let out a big breath and finish cleaning Babe's hoof with the brush.

"Awesome," David says. "Walking on stones like that can bruise a horse or cause an infection." He kicks the stone out of the way so Babe doesn't step on it again. "I bet these guys haven't seen a farrier in months. See how her hooves are chipped and uneven?"

"Can I ask a dumb question?" I ask.

"I specialize in dumb questions," he says with a grin.

"What's a farrier?"

"Farriers are in charge of hooves, kind of a mix between a blacksmith and hoof doctor. All the horses at Quinn's stables see Angela regularly; she clips, files, and balances their hooves and replaces the shoes. The horses love her. Mr. Quinn calls her the 'horseshoe master.'"

"Maybe we should be calling ourselves "pony ride masters!" I say.

We get the grooming finished just in time. Jules comes around the corner of the store leading the line of kids who are ready to ride. Not surprisingly, Sophie is in the front. She's taught the pony song to her new friends, and they sing it so loudly that they drown out the traffic noise. Jules has everyone sit in a neat line by the planters and then joins us.

"We can't use Buster?" she asks.

"Dr. Gabe said not to," I explain.

"How do I explain that to the kids?" she asks.

David is tacking up Babe. "They've all gotten boo-boos, they'll understand."

"You could have them make get-well cards for him," I suggest.

"Good idea," she says. "Brenna left a message saying she'll be here soon. Sunita will be here later. Her family's having a big Sunday dinner."

"You better bring Sophie over here," I say. "If she sings that song any louder, she's going to hurt herself."

Chapter Fifteen

David and I take turns walking Babe and her rider around the corral. Every five minutes I ask David to check what time it is; one o'clock is coming way too fast.

But when one comes, Gus does not arrive. One oh-five, one ten . . .

"Did someone say there's a lame pony around here?"

Out of the back door of the store comes my father and Dr. Gabe, who's carrying an emergency medical kit.

My heart skips, then falls.

"Oh, no," I say. "The Labradoodle?

"He's still in surgery," Dr. Gabe says.

"But—"

"Dr. Mac and the girls got home just after we hung up," he explains. "Both Zoe and Maggie woke up with a stomach bug. I assisted Dr. Mac with the surgery on the Labradoodle, then she sent me here to check out Buster."

"Anything I can do to help?" Dad asks.

"Just keep your eyes open for Gus," I say. "He's supposed to be here any minute."

As Dad walks away, Dr. Gabe introduces himself to Buster, gently smoothing his mane while the pony smells him.

"I thought you couldn't treat him without Gus's permission," I say.

"That's right," he says. "But I can certainly have a look at him." He takes a stethoscope out of the kit and listens to the pulse point behind Buster's front leg and then listens to the sounds in his belly. After he checks Buster's gums, he runs his hand along Buster's side and down his right front leg. "Okay, there, buddy, are you in the mood to show me that hoof of yours?"

Buster must feel reassured by Dr. Gabe's tone of voice and confident touch because he lifts his hoof out of the bucket.

"Hmmm." Dr. Gabe frowns as he feels Buster's lower leg.

"It smelled awful this morning," I said.

"That smell usually indicates an abscess." Dr. Gabe puts his thumb and finger on the lower part of the leg. "I'm feeling a strong thumping digital pulse here at the fetlock," he says. "We don't feel a strong pulse here unless there is an infection in his foot." He finally lifts Buster's hoof. The pony shudders, but lets the doc check out the bottom of the hoof.

"It's definitely very tender here. Do you want to see?" Dr. Gabe asks.

I peek over the vet's shoulder to see what's happening. The underside of Buster's hoof looks very different than Babe's. It's moist and mushy and smells bad, too. Dr. Gabe cleans it out with a a small hooked instrument that he calls a hoof pick and tells me about the parts of the hoof. "The structure in the middle is the frog. This is the hoof wall, the hoof capsule, and the white line, which holds the areas together." He leans in to look closer.

"I don't see any stones," I say.

"I'm also looking for punctures or cracks; openings where bacteria could have entered, causing this infection. The hoof has an abscess—that much is clear. They're common in horses and ponies and really hurt, which is why Buster suddenly couldn't walk."

Dr. Gabe uses a set of hoof testers, squeezing the metal prongs around the hoof. Buster cooperates until Dr. Gabe squeezes the hoof tester on one spot, then Buster pulls his foot away.

"Yep," Dr. Gabe says. "See there? Buster is letting us know where it hurts. When an infection digs in, the horse's body fights back by sending white blood cells to the area. They form pus. If the pus builds up in the body, it causes inflammation and pain. As the tissue around the wound dies and the pus leaks, you get that stench."

"How did it get infected?" I ask.

"He could have stepped on a nail from a thrown shoe, or a bit of stone or dirt could have worked its way into the hoof. A horse will be fine one moment, then suddenly seem completely lame the next."

"That's how Buster was yesterday!" I exclaim. "Totally fine, then suddenly limping."

"We need to find out if Buster is up to date on his tetanus shots," he says. "An infection like this almost guarantees exposure to the bacteria that cause tetanus, and that disease can kill an animal. That's why it's so important to clean and check the hooves. There's an old saying: 'No hoof, no horse.'"

He gently eases Buster's hoof onto the pavement.

"The good news is, abscesses are easy to treat. He'll feel better as soon as I drain it, and it should heal with no problem if the hoof is kept clean and allowed to continue to drain."

"Sounds like there's bad news, too," I say.

"Sadly, there is." He stands up. "I need Gus's permission to drain the abscess."

"But he caused it, right? He doesn't take good care of them; that's why Buster is sick!"

Dr. Gabe pets Buster's neck. "Even ponies who are treated wonderfully can develop abscesses. The law requires that before I help an animal I have to get 'informed consent.' The owner has to understand what I want to do to his animal, and he has to give me his permission. If that doesn't happen, I can lose my license to be a veterinarian."

"Glad you know it," says a harsh voice.

I look up, startled, to find that Gus is standing behind us.

"Hand over that lead," Gus demands. "Time for these ponies to leave."

Chapter Sixteen

You must be Gus." Dr. Gabe extends a hand. "I'm Gabe Donovan, from Dr. Mac's Place. I've heard a lot about you. The kids are really enjoying your ponies."

Gus eyes the doc suspiciously but shakes his hand. "Kids always love ponies; that's why it's a good business."

Standing by the corral, Jules raises her hands and gives an exaggerated shrug, trying to ask me what she should do. Gus is busy untying Buster's lead. I pretend to hold a phone to my ear, and she nods. Thank goodness for our twin connection. She has a quick conversation with David, then sprints toward the store.

I try to keep my voice calm and friendly. "It's a shame you're going to lose so much money."

"What are you talking about?" Gus grumbles.

"Buster has an abscessed hoof," Dr. Gabe explains. "He won't be able to work unless it's treated."

"Ponies heal up naturally," Gus says. "They don't need interference from the likes of you."

Dr. Gabe bristles but calmly replies, "Well, that can sometimes be the case, but in my opinion, when an abscess reaches this point—"

"I don't give a hoot about your opinion!" Gus says. He points at David and hollers, "Rides are over! Get that kid off of Babe!"

The parents of the little boy on Babe's back approach the corral to talk to David. I sure hope he figures out the right thing to say to them.

"Horse doctors are too expensive anyway," Gus mutters.

"But it's free!" I blurt out. "My dad will pay the bill."

This is a total lie, and it could be a complete disaster, but it's the only thing I can think of. We have to keep Gus here as long as possible.

"Free?" Gus asks.

Dr. Gabe looks at me, one eyebrow raised. He

has to know that I'm not telling the truth, but he plays along. "Hard to turn down an offer like that," he says.

Oh, man. I'm gonna be in so much trouble later. I'll probably be babysitting and doing odd jobs for the rest of my life to pay this vet bill. But I can't think about that now.

"Well, if it won't cost me anything—" Gus says. "Guess I shouldn't look a gift horse in the mouth. Go ahead, fix him up."

"Excellent!" Dr. Gabe replies.

As the last family leaves the corral, David ties Babe's lead and heads for the door, making the phone-call sign that I gave Jules a few minutes ago. I'm not sure who he's going to call, or why, but I hope it helps.

"You." Gus jerks his chin at me. "Take down the corral while the doc is working."

"I um . . . can't," I stall.

"Why not?" Gus demands.

"I need Josh's help draining the abscess," Dr. Gabe says, giving me a strange wink that I don't quite understand. "He's my assistant, after all."

"I am?" I ask, stomach flopping. Gus gives me a funny look. "I am!" I repeat quickly, trying to sound enthusiastic. My heart is beating fast. I feel a little proud that Dr. Gabe called me his assistant, but that whole "draining the abscess" thing makes me want to run and hide.

"Well, I haven't got all day," Gus says. "If you're gonna fix up Buster, you'd better get to it."

"I just need to see Buster's medical records," Dr. Gabe says.

"I don't have that stuff with me," Gus says.

"You don't keep copies in your truck?" Dr. Gabe asks.

"I just said that, didn't I?" Gus asks. The angry tone of his voice makes Buster lay his ears back.

"How long have you owned Buster?" Dr. Gabe asks.

"I dunno. Six, seven years."

Dr. Gabe says takes a small notebook out of his medical kit. "Best guess, when was his last tetanus shot?"

"Can't remember," Gus says. "Just give him another one. That'll be free, too, right?"

"There are different protocols depending on when he was last vaccinated," Dr. Gabe explains calmly and gently, as if talking to a child.

"I don't have time for this," Gus says, looks agitated now. "We need to get on the road."

"Okay, okay, no worries." Dr. Gabe turns to me. "Are you ready to assist, Josh?"

I say, "Yes," but I'm thinking, *No!*

Dr. Gabe gives me a squirt of hand sanitizer and pulls a few things out of his bag, including surgical gloves for both of us. I struggle to pull the gloves on, trying not to think about the fact that I'm about to help with a medical procedure. The problem with trying not to think about something is that it becomes the only thing you can think about.

"I'm going to break down the corral," Gus says. "Hope you're done by the time I am."

Dr. Gabe waits for the pony handler to get out of earshot. "You weren't kidding about him, were you?" He sighs. "Let's do our best here."

I hold Buster's bridle and stroke his nose while Dr. Gabe gets Buster to bend his leg so the doc can get to work. He uses a hoof pick to scrape away a soft bit of Buster's infected hoof.

"There! See that blackish section?" Dr. Gabe asks.

My stomach flops, flips, and flops again. I breathe deeply through my mouth, swallow hard, and look. Wow. It is disgusting.

Dr. Gabe picks up a scalpel. "I bet the abscess is right here," Dr. Gabe says as he lances the spot.

As soon as he punctures the surface, nasty-smelling yellow gunk oozes out. Ugh.

Deep breath, deep breath! I stare at the white star on Buster's forehead and try to settle my stomach. The poor pony probably thinks I'm nuts. I glance at the infected hoof—*Deep breath! Deep breath!*—and look back at Buster. The tightness around his eyes has already faded. I think about how Buster's pain was so much worse than any of my stupid nausea, and he looks better already. Having the abscess lanced must have really helped—and knowing that I helped Buster makes the gross stuff easier to stomach. I take one more deep breath and look at the hoof again. This time, I don't have to look away.

"There we go," Dr. Gabe says, sounding satisfied. "Purulent material."

"Purulent?" I ask.

"It means this fluid has pus in it," Dr. Gabe says.

"A gross word for a gross thing," I say.

"Yep." The doc chuckles. "Hand me that bottle of cleaning solution, please."

I pet and distract Buster as Dr. Gabe cleans the abscessed area.

"Now one of those medicated pads," he says, pointing to the pack he needs with his elbow. He presses a pad on the bottom of the hoof and more pus leaks out. He repeats this process several times, using a clean pad each time. When he presses the fourth pad on the hoof, a little blood seeps out, but no pus.

"Can you come around and hold this?" he asks. "I need to get the tape ready."

I brace Buster's knee with my leg and press the pad against the hoof. "Tape? Won't that just fall off as soon as he takes a step?"

"This tape is specially made for horses," he says as he tears off a strip. "It will keep that pad in place and protect the wound." He wraps the pad quickly and straightens up. "You can let go of his foot now."

We watch as Buster gingerly puts the injured foot on the ground. He shakes his mane.

"Nice," says Dr. Gabe. "Look at the difference in him already."

I don't answer because I know that it won't last. Gus has finished unpinning the corral panels and is driving his pickup truck into the parking lot. Babe is tied to the horse trailer. As soon as Gus gets out of the truck, she lifts her tail and deposits a poop pile.

"My thoughts exactly," I mutter.

A second pickup truck enters the lot.

"Did Gus bring a friend?" Dr. Gabe asks.

"I don't think he has any friends," I say. "It's probably a customer for the store."

But the truck skips all the parking places, drives up to us, and parks. A tall, thin man with a bushy black beard gets out of the driver's seat. I recognize him—it's Brenna's dad. Out of the passenger's side steps a man about my dad's age who's dressed in fishing gear. I've never seen him before. The second man flips forward the passenger's-side seat so the people in the back can get out.

"We made it!" yells Brenna, pumping her fists.

She's followed by Sunita, who says, "I can't believe it!"

Dr. Gabe walks up to Mr. Lake and greets him. "Good to see you. What are you doing here?"

Mr. Lake points to the guy in the fishing gear. "Have you met Gary Snyder?"

Gary Snyder reaches out to shake the vet's hand. "I'm Animal Control," he quietly says.

Brenna raises her fists again, triumphant.

"Nice to meet you. This is my new assistant, Josh," Dr. Gabe says. "He needs to talk to you about these ponies."

Chapter Seventeen

Everything happens so fast I feel like I'm on a roller coaster. As I'm explaining to Mr. Snyder everything that has happened, Jules comes out of the house waving a handful of papers: the responses to the e-mail I sent out last night. Mom is with Jules, and she looks pretty worried. Brenna's dad introduces her to Mr. Snyder, who starts going through the printed e-mails.

He flips through the pages quickly, but I catch a few phrases.

Never, never, NEVER hire Gustav Blusterfeld.

. . . the most incompetent, dishonest worker I have ever met.

. . . The sad thing is, his sister, Gloria, was a top-notch pony

handler. But when she passed away and Gus took over, everything changed.

. . . Dishonest business practices, driving without a license, and mistreatment of his ponies, among other things.

. . . Cruel, neglectful, and just plain mean.

. . . I wanted to press charges, but he left town . . .

Mr. Snyder looks at Dr. Gabe. "What have you seen?"

"There's certainly been evidence of neglect. Ask him for the vaccination records and the name of his vet," Dr. Gabe says. "I guarantee you'll come up empty."

"Stay here," Mr. Snyder tells us.

The Animal Control officer walks over to Gus, shows the pony handler his identification, and starts talking, but they are standing too far away for us to hear them.

David jogs out to us. "What's going on?" he asks.

"Showdown at the Wrenches and Roses Corral!" I say.

"You can't do that!" Gus hollers at Mr. Snyder.

Buster shifts his feet nervously, and I reach out to pet and reassure him.

Mr. Snyder says something quietly, but Gus steps up to him and pokes his finger in the middle of his chest. My dad and Dr. Gabe both tense up.

"Do you think we're needed?" the doc asks Dad.

"Nope." Dad points to the police cruiser that's turning into the parking lot. "Looks like the cavalry just arrived."

It takes more than an hour before everything is sorted out. At first, Gus was yelling at Mr. Snyder and the police officer, and Mom didn't want the Vet Volunteers to watch or even listen. I could tell she wasn't too happy with Gus's cursing. It got a little scary, but Dad convinced her that we were old enough to learn about things like this.

After Mr. Snyder had taken a look at Buster and his hoof, he told Gus sternly, "You can't work an animal to the point of lameness. And from the looks of those e-mails, this isn't the first time this has happened. Normally, I might be able to let you go with a warning and a fine, but this has gone beyond my jurisdiction." And then the policeman took over. It was so cool! Just like one of the cop shows that Dad and I watch.

The police officer put handcuffs on Gus and made him sit in the back of his squad car. By then, Gus looked a little sad, like he'd given up, and I almost felt sorry for him. But mostly, I was just happy that Buster was okay.

Meanwhile, Dr. Gabe brought Babe over to

where we were standing with Buster. Now that Buster had been treated and was with Babe again, he was like a brand-new pony, nuzzling Babe and nickering softly. The whole time David was announcing what we were watching like it was a tennis match, making everyone crack up.

I sat on the ground next to Sunita. We didn't talk to each other, but it was a comfortable silence, and that made me feel pretty good.

After chatting a bit longer with Mr. Snyder, the officer tipped his hat in our direction, got in his car, and drove off.

Mr. Snyder had all the answers we'd been dying for.

"Gus has a half-dozen warrants out for his arrest—for everything from theft to drunk driving," he says. "Plus, his truck isn't registered or insured, and Gus had his license to drive taken away years ago. When he realized that he was going to be arrested, he was finally honest about the ponies: they haven't been seen by a vet or gotten any vaccinations since his sister died."

"So what happens now?" I ask. "What about Buster and Babe?"

"I gave him a choice," Mr. Snyder says. "He could let me take the animals and I would send him the bill for their care and boarding. Instead, he offered to give the animals away."

"But where do we put them?" I ask. "They can't stay here. We can take care of a couple of bunnies, but we definitely can't handle two ponies. Plus, Buster needs to go someplace where his abscess can be watched."

David points at me. "You are a worrywart with horse sense, Josh. Mr. Quinn is gonna love you."

"What are you talking about?" I ask.

"I called him when I went inside. Your mom told me that your dad had already called the police, so I told Mr. Quinn that there was a good chance the ponies were about to be homeless."

"What did he say?"

"There's an old shed behind the stables that he's been using for equipment. It's kind of beat-up and dirty, but he said if we clean it out, the ponies could stay there until a better home is found for them. He even offered to call a friend who runs a therapy-riding program—Helping Hands School for Special Riders. He thinks Buster and Babe would be perfect for it."

I blink, trying to sort it all out. "Mr. Quinn's going to save them?"

"No, dork." David punches my shoulder. "You're the one who saved them."

Sunita nods her head. "He's right, Josh. You noticed when Buster was sick. You did all the research; you pulled everything together."

I start blushing so hard my cheeks feel like they're on fire.

"And you showed me a real willingness to help and to learn," Dr. Gabe says.

"Well, thanks," I say, "but . . ." There's one last thing I'm worried about. I swallow. "Dad? I kind of told Gus that we would pay for Buster's treatment today. I know I shouldn't have, but it was the only way to get him to agree to Dr. Gabe's help." I jam my hands into my pockets and keep my eyes on the ground. I can't help feeling like I screwed up again.

But Dad's voice doesn't sound angry.

"Hmmm, is that so?" he asks. I look up. He's exchanging a glance with Dr. Gabe, and there's a twinkle in his eye.

Dr. Gabe clears his throat. "You know, John, I could use Josh's help. He's done a great job assisting me with Buster, and it's the busy season at the farms in the area. Lots of newborn animals that need tending. A few hours on the weekends for the next few weeks, and we can call it even. What do you say?"

Dad smiles and nods. "I'd say that sounds just

fine. Seems like my son was a real help today."

Now I'm blushing even harder.

I punch David's shoulder. "This dork here helped, too. In fact, we did this together, all of us."

"That's enough of that," David says, rubbing his shoulder. "Next thing you know, the girls are going to want a group hug."

"Not a hug," Brenna says, "but we do need a picture. Can you take one, Daddy, please?"

"Sure thing."

Brenna pulls out her camera and hands it to her dad as we line up: Jules, Sunita, Buster, me, Babe, David, and Brenna. We put our arms around each other and look at the camera.

"Okay, everybody," says Mr. Lake. "Say 'Vet Volunteers!'"

Pony Care and Fun Horse Facts

By J. J. MACKENZIE, D.V.M.

Humans and horses have had a long relationship throughout history, and horses rely on humans to provide proper care. Whether you are a horse owner or merely enjoy a pony ride from time to time, here are some easy ways to help horses, as well as some surprising things you might not know about our equine friends.

Basic Care

Horses must have fresh, clean water at all times, as well as adequate food and shelter. A quick glance over a horse for any cuts or bruises is a good way to notice small injuries before they get worse. It is very important that hooves are kept clean and that horseshoes are in good shape, otherwise the horse could go lame.

Fun Facts

Horses are vegetarians! That's right, horses are herbivores and do not eat any meat.

Humans domesticated horses around 3500 B.C. We've used these amazing animals for work, play, battle, and more for thousands of years.

You can determine a horse's age by looking at its teeth! As a horse ages, it wears its teeth by grazing, and you can estimate how old it is by the grooves in the horse's teeth. And horses lose their baby teeth, just like humans do.

There are many different types of horses who lead very different lives, from wild horses on Assateague Island to race horses in the Kentucky Derby.

How You Can Help and Learn More

If you live near a farm or a riding school, see if you can ask a farmer for a barn tour, or sign up for a riding lesson.

If you suspect that a horse is not being well cared for, ask an adult for help.

Read more horse books! *Black Beauty* is a must-read classic for any horse fan.

More horse resources can be found at:

http://animals.nationalgeographic.com/animals/mammals/horse/

http://horses.about.com/

http://www.humanesociety.org/animals/horses/

Join the Vet Volunteers on another adventure!

Chapter One

"You're dumping me again, Mom."

"Zoe, don't be dramatic."

Mom sits at Gran's kitchen table and doesn't take her eyes off me. I lean against the counter, cross my arms, and roll my eyes to the ceiling.

"Zoe, it would be different if we were filming this movie only during the summer. But it's going to take months. You can't be out of middle school that long. Once summer starts, you can visit me for a week or two on set in Vancouver."

Visit. What does that mean? I guess Mom expects to be in Canada through the summer, but how long after that? And why can't I spend the whole summer with her?

Mom takes a tiny bite out of her Pop-Tart and washes it down with a gulp of coffee. She doesn't usually eat sugary stuff like that, but here at Gran's house there's no organic yogurt in the fridge, and the bananas on her counter are rounding the corner from deep brown to black. Pop-Tarts for breakfast it is. I'm not even remotely hungry, though. Mom wrinkles her nose and takes another bite.

We just arrived late last night and Mom is already leaving again. She's continuing on to New York City. We used to live there together. Then I moved to Ambler before joining Mom in California, and now it's back to Ambler again—for me, at least. In New York, Mom is meeting once more with the movie's costume designer and checking in with some of her old soap-opera friends. They're my friends, too, and I don't see why I can't at least make the trip to New York before settling in to life in Ambler, Pennsylvania, again.

I try one more time. "Why can't I just spend the weekend in New York with you before you fly to Vancouver? I can take the train back here by myself, you know I can."

"We've gone over and over this. You know I promised your grandmother that I would deliver you here. New York will be much too hectic. I wouldn't have time to have fun with you; I have too much to fit in before we start shooting—"

"But it's spring break here this week!" I say. "I wouldn't even be missing school."

"Which is why this is so perfect. You'll have a little time to settle back in with Gran and Maggie before having to start school again."

Mom gets up from the table and hugs me. A car horn blares out front.

"That's my cab. Listen, Zoe, we'll check in with each other every day or so. Once I'm on set it might be a little more time between calls or emails. But I promise we'll stay in touch, okay? Of course we will." Mom squeezes me hard and kisses my cheek. Her breath smells like strong coffee and even stronger peppermint. She gathers up her bags and sweeps toward the door.

"Tell my mother good-bye for me. I can't wait around until she's finished with whichever four-legged friend she's tending to now!" She waves as she leaves.

"I love you," I hear Mom sing out after the door has closed behind her.

I sigh. Stranded again. Left behind by Mom because she has bigger plans than me. I guess I might as well go back to bed. I'm still pretty tired from traveling, and I don't exactly feel ready to face this new—er, old—life. I'm heading back to my old bedroom when I hear my name. It's my cousin Maggie. I can hear her talking to a boy and a girl whose voices I don't recognize. I pause, standing behind the kitchen door separating Gran's house from her vet clinic.

"Late," Maggie says. "Really late. Gran picked up Zoe and Aunt Rose from the airport after midnight. Their plane was delayed. Gran let me stay up so I could say hi to them. I think Aunt Rose has already left. She had to be in New York City this morning."

"Wow. It must be a big change, going from Hollywood back to living in Ambler. Does she seem different to you?" the girl asks.

"Zoe? Not much. Even jet-lagged Zoe is pretty dramatic." The way Maggie says it I'm not sure if she means that in a good way or not. I love her, but Maggie and I haven't always gotten along.

"But who knows. Gran pretty much sent us right to bed," Maggie continues. "Then she and Aunt Rose stayed up talking. I think Zoe is still sleeping, but you'll meet her at some point today."

"Do you look alike?" the girl asks.

"They're cousins, not twin sisters!" the boy says.

"We look nothing alike," Maggie begins. "Well, she does have a little MacKenzie red in her long blond hair. But no freckles like me. And she dresses . . . she dresses . . . well, different. You'll see."

What does Maggie mean by "*different*"? I just look neat and tidy. Okay, and rather stylish. I think about the three extra suitcases I begged Mom to let me bring, brimming with new jeans, sparkly shirts, and an embarrassing number of shoes. Maggie, I am sure, must look like her usual red-headed, flannel shirt–wearing self. She could look so much better if she just took a minute with her hair or cared a tiny bit about her clothes—and not just about whether they were clean or not. But all Maggie cares about is basketball and animals. Which are both great, but maybe she'll finally let me give her some style tips this time around. Maybe.

"How long will she be staying?" the girl asks.

"I have no idea," Maggie says with a funny voice. I wish I had seen her face when she said that. "Maybe the rest of the school year and the whole summer? Her mom's filming in Vancouver will probably take about that long," she continues.

"I can't believe her mom is a movie star," the girl says.

"I don't think you could call her a movie star, but she's an actress, anyway."

What?? I would definitely call my mother a movie star! Well, okay, maybe not yet. But she is a star of this movie, anyway.

"My aunt is really pretty," Maggie adds. "Zoe is, too."

Aw, that's nice. I'm about to go show them what I look like when I hear the boy ask, "Are you happy she's back? Will it be weird to share your grandmother again?"

Yeah, I sure do want to hear the answer to this one.

I listen closely. I hear only the metallic sound of cage doors opening and closing. The kids must have moved into the recovery room to clean cages. It's Saturday morning, and I know that is on Gran's Vet Volunteers to-do list.

I open the door a tiny bit to try to hear better. I know they can't see me here, but their voices are still muffled.

"Are you coming in to help, or are you going to stand at the door all day?" The voice startles me. Standing behind me is Dr. J. J. MacKenzie, owner of Dr. Mac's Place Veterinary Clinic to everybody here in Ambler, Pennsylvania. But to Maggie and me, she's just Gran, wonder woman caretaker of orphaned granddaughters. Maggie, fulltime since her parents died in a car crash. And me, any time my mom's acting career is more important than I am.

"Zoe?" Gran examines me. "Still sleepy?" she asks.

"No, I'm fine."

"Welcome back," Gran says, holding the door wide.

"It's good to *be* back," I say. I walk in with a small smile, but I don't really mean it. There's a lot about Ambler to love, but right now, it just feels like a place where I keep ending up—a place that isn't my real home.

" 'Bout time you showed up to clean," Maggie says, her head deep in a large kitten crate on the floor. Through the cage wires I can see her grin.

"Hi, I'm Josh Darrow," says the boy in the corner. He's about my age and has friendly brown eyes and slightly curly brown hair. He has on the gloves Gran makes us wear when we clean around here.

"This is Jules, my sister. We're the newest Vet Volunteers." Josh sweeps his yellow-gloved arm toward a girl holding a teeny gray kitten. The brother and sister look about the same age. She has the same brown eyes and the same color hair. Maybe they're twins?

"Hi," the girl says shyly.

"Hi. I'm Zoe," I say, like that isn't obvious. Of course they know who I am. Still, everyone just smiles. Even Gran.

"Okay," Gran begins, "if we're finished with the

cleaning, let's have Maggie and Josh exercise our boarder dogs and Jules can show Zoe what we're doing with those kittens." Gran moves on to a mountain of paperwork on the counter. It's a mess. Some things never change.

"We have some little-bitties here," Jules says, bending over Maggie's now-clean kitten crate and settling the gray kitten into it. "Three of them are on bottles now, but not the two littlest ones. Have you used this before?" Jules holds up the eyedropper that we use to feed the smallest, weakest animals.

"I have," I say, heading to the sinks to scrub my hands, wrists, and forearms. It's all about safety at Dr. Mac's Place, and safety begins with cleanliness, as Gran always says.

Jules and I work in silence for a while. We feed the two tiny kittens with the eyedropper and the three healthier kittens with small bottles. Jules had filled all the bottles with formula and set them on the warmer pad before we began. After each kitten is fed, we wipe the corners of their eyes, their mouths, and noses with a small, moistened gauze pad. We check their fur all over to be sure they are clean and don't have any mites or fleas. And then we tuck each one back in under the heat lamp in the clean kitten crate.